SUN CHARA

Greetings from southern California! I'm a teacher turned actor/writer and have appeared on stage and film in How the Other Half Loves, General Hospital, and McGee & Me. The showbiz background comes in handy with speaking engagements, judging RWA contests, and judging the Emmys. I have a Master of Arts Degree, and I'm a member of the Screen Actors Guild and Romance Writers of America. Globetrotting for lore (once, on an excursion amidst the pyramids in the Valley of the Kings, a gentleman offered fifteen camels for my hand…now had it been race horses…) while keeping tabs on Hollywood leads, I love creating stories of pure passion with global thrills!

Follow me on Twitter @sunchara3.

Manhattan Millionaire's Cinderella

SUN CHARA

Harper*Impulse* an imprint of
HarperCollins*Publishers Ltd*
77–85 Fulham Palace Road
Hammersmith, London W6 8JB

www.harpercollins.co.uk

A Paperback Original 2014

First published in Great Britain in ebook format by HarperImpulse 2013

Copyright © Sun Chara 2013

Cover Images © Shutterstock.com

Sun Chara asserts the moral right to
be identified as the author of this work

A catalogue record for this book
is available from the British Library

ISBN: 978-0-00-755964-0

This novel is entirely a work of fiction.
The names, characters and incidents portrayed in it are
the work of the author's imagination. Any resemblance to
actual persons, living or dead, events or localities is
entirely coincidental.

Set in Minion by FMG

To my sweet mom, bros Joe and Harry and family, and the beautiful people of Cyprus, England and across the globe … you shine!

Mega thanks to creative genius, Jordi Alba for his generosity with the giant ad screens, and to World-class filmmaker, Gerard Alba for the favor of an amazing book trailer!

A super nova thanks to my wonderful editor Charlotte Ledger who spoke words of wonder: 'I really feel it's meant to be having picked you out of SYTYCW!' Wow!

Bunches of thanks to the best ever publishing team at HarperImpulse … you are magical!

And to everyone who has a dream, Never Give Up! 'With God all things are possible.'

CHAPTER ONE

Cade Sloan—Manhattan's hotshot bachelor on the brink of bankruptcy.

Cade read the headline and hurled the newspaper into the trashcan, the taunting words searing his brain. Prowling back and forth his high-rise office, he paused mid stride and zoned in on his secretary, who sat ramrod straight, her fingers flying across the computer keyboard.

"Ms. McLow—" The words dissolved on his tongue, and he scratched his head. What was her name anyway?

"Ms. McLow—" He cleared his throat and tried again. "Ms.—"

"McLowsky." She lifted a shapely brow and tossed him a glance through her coke-bottle thick lenses, a blush on her cheeks. "Nina McLowsky."

Did she just click her tongue in disapproval?

Just his luck. She came with attitude.

"Of course." He swiped a finger around his shirt collar, and his chest tightened. "Nina McLowsky." Scrambling to regroup, he seized the coffee-mate from the counter and filled a cup with coffee.

She looked like she had walked out of a 1950s Norman Rockwell painting, the epitome of diplomacy and efficiency. He stroked his

1

throat, and then shook his head, amazed. He was actually flirting with the idea of a merger …with her.

At least with her there'd be no emotional tantrums. The thought had him breaking out in a sweat. He never let any woman get close enough to get a glimpse beneath the surface, to know what made him tick. 'Never trust a woman,' was his motto.

A cab horn blared amidst the congested traffic on Madison Avenue and ripped through his thoughts. He flinched in annoyance.

He hadn't felt this out of his depth since he was a boy, and he had vowed never to feel like this again. And he was running out of options. His global real estate investments were about to tank. He had to score a mega hit or he was going to cave. Fast.

And that rankled his pride.

"Here you go." He plopped the coffee cup on her desk, and a huff of air burst from his mouth, ruffling a wisp at her temple.

She squinted at the steaming brew, then up at him, her baby blues all innocence and perplexity. "Thank you."

His gut flexed. He frowned and dismissed the unsettling feeling. "Careful, it's hot."

She peered at him above her thick lenses, a hint of a smile on her mouth, her fingers never missing a beat. Maybe if he focused on the dimple on her cheek, he could go through with the transaction.

"Take a moment, Ms. McLowsky." The smell of caffeine gave him a boost, and latching onto his own mug, he shot her his killer smile.

"Sir?"

"Well…uh…" he began, words sticking in his throat. "Drink up."

"Yes, sir." She picked up the steaming cup, blew on the liquid and took a sip, fixing her gaze on him over the rim.

Was that a glint of amusement in her eyes?

She blinked and it was gone. "Is that it, sir?" She set the cup on the desk.

"No." He lifted his mug to his lips, took a gulp of the black brew and scorched his tongue. He swore, a muffled sound.

She heard, and raised that well-defined eyebrow again.

"There's a new position in the company." He stepped closer and hitching up his jean-clad leg, propped his hip on the corner of her desk. "You're the best match."

"What is it?"

"A merger, of sorts."

At thirty-three, Cade was not averse to a challenge; it was the coercion tactics his uncle still used that he abhorred. His uncle. His lifelong nemesis, whom he'd booted from the boardroom, now tossed him a curve to the tune of three million—problem was the deal included a stipulation to muzzle…er… marry him off.

Cade was under no illusions that his uncle's offer was iced with ulterior motives, but, in no position to refuse, he had to take the bait. A pittance, but it'd swing him from the red into the black, and buy him some time. He'd expand his global holdings, complete the mega development in Cyprus, triple his profits and—his heart turned to stone—catch the hacker embezzling company funds.

The con was about to demolish Cade into a heap of rubble. He had to do something.

He scrubbed the stubble on his jaw, and his gaze swerved to *her*. He'd racked his brain for the perfect candidate, and Ms. Straitlaced, now staring up at him with half parted lips, best fit the bill—no complications.

She licked her lips, and then nipped the bottom one with her teeth.

His gut got unhinged with that strange feeling again. He yanked his gaze away from her mouth and plummeted into the ocean of her eyes. He bounced off, aimed lower and got socked in the belly. Beneath her colorless dress, her breasts rose and fell with every breath she took, and he imagined—

Get a grip, man. Oh yeah. Freud would get a big chuckle outta that.

Cade cleared his throat. "A marr—" He coughed, and forced the words out. "A marriage proposal." A noose around his neck.

"What?" She gaped at him as though he'd gone bonkers, then her stiff discipline kicked in. "A *market* proposal, sir?"

"Nice try." Somehow, he'd outmaneuver his uncle's ploy to get him hitched, but first, he had to get his hands on the dough.

"Matrimony." He scowled. "It'd be a promotion. Higher salary...perks...company car...me."

She laughed, but there was a nervous tingle in it. "I don't qualify, sir."

"Indeed, you do." He'd checked her out and she came out squeaky clean. Lived with her cat, bicycled in Central Park on weekends, no boyfriend, a mother in Los Angeles; Her father, a former employee of the company before Cade's takeover, unaccounted for. He curled his lip in distaste. Divorce, no doubt.

"Marry...you?!"

Heck, did she have to sound so shocked? Plenty of sophisticates would snatch at his proposal. He palmed his nape. But this business model called for specific criteria—and he was looking at her. "Yeah."

"Why?"

"Because—"

"I don't even like you."

That cut through his thick hide and pricked his pride. He shrugged.

"You don't have to."

She giggled, and the sound booted him with a delicious zap.

"Strictly a business transaction." He pointed to himself then to her. "Mutually beneficial."

"No, thank you."

Aww, man, there she went barricading herself behind her prim and proper façade. He had to knock her defenses down and clinch the deal.

"Would a percentage of three million change your mind?"

"Very funny." She shifted in her chair and resumed typing.

"Okay." He slid off the desk. "If you change your mind—"

The phone rang.

Nina picked up the receiver and sized him up over the rim of her glasses. Sexual energy vibrated from him, a catalyst to her own. Good reason to keep her distance. "I'll see if Mr. Sloan's avail—"

He grabbed the phone from her so quickly, a whoosh of hot air singed the back of her hand.

"Sloan," he barked, making the room shrink. "No way in hell." He paced the floor, the muscles in his back contracting. A scowl creased his otherwise handsome features. It was a face that had women lining up and gossip hounds salivating after him.

A shiver shimmied up her spine.

Cade Sloan gobbled girls like her for appetizers, spat them out and moved onto the entrée. Breath whipped from her lips, and she twitched her nose. No way would she be another notch on this stud's belt.

Nina had her life mapped out. And it did not include her sexy boss who had just propositioned her. She fiddled with her pearl earring, and her gaze strayed back to him.

"Not my type," she murmured beneath her breath.

He heard and cocked a brow, his eyes shuttering.

Heat—his heat shot into her. Perspiration dampened her skin and a droplet meandered between her breasts. She pulled a tissue from the Kleenex box and dabbed her upper lip.

He was much too dangerous.

Lethal…to her.

What if he was behind her father's disappearance? Her father was a former employee.

"I need more time." Already having dismissed her, he glanced over her head at the New York skyline visible through the wide expanse of glass of one wall. "Three days." Gold flecks in his eyes glittered, then he crashed the phone down, tension riddling his broad shoulders as he let out a deep breath of frustration. He strode to the door, paused, and tossed over his shoulder. "Think it over, Ms. McLowsky."

"Why?"

"Because...er...you've got the stellar qualifications stipulated for the position."

She shook her head, and a curl dared play fickle at her temple. She batted it away with the back of her hand, and resisted the temptation he dangled before her. "I'm flattered, but—"

"No flattery intended." He laughed. It sounded like a snort and made her bristle with indignation. "Cold, hard cash. Plenty of it." About to step across the threshold, he paused in stride, one foot firmly set on her turf, the other about to land in his office.

"How much?" Nina blushed to the roots of her hair knotted at her nape. Had she actually uttered those words? She swallowed. Okay, he was serving up a deal that didn't cross a girl's desk every day.

Wouldn't hurt to get the particulars, would it? It could be her ticket out of a nine to five and enable her to open her lingerie boutique before her thirtieth birthday which was just months away. She'd achieve financial independence and go full force after the creepola who lured her father away, leaving her mother a broken heap.

Nina took a breath and shook herself from her lapse into the past. Removing her glasses, she blinked at Cade's back, and a funny sensation fluttered in her stomach. She ignored it. Mustn't skip lunch again.

Working through lunch and after hours afforded her time to search for answers. Now, here was the boss handing her a prime opportunity to get them. She propped her eyeglasses back on her nose. Being linked to Cade Sloan would give her access to confidential files that might give her the coup to her father's whereabouts.

Would she dare? And if she did, could she go through with it?

Her palms grew moist, and she swiped them on her loose fitting dress.

A nervous giggle slipped between her lips. Would it be so awful, if it got her closer to her goal?

But what if you fall for him? She rolled her eyes. Not a chance in hell.

"Fifty thousand." Cade turned, setting both feet on the floorboards, and held her gaze.

"Wha-at?" Her mind filled with possibilities before his words had her clambering to refocus.

"Fifty grand."

"That's pocket change." She retorted, surprising herself. She must be dimwitted to even debate this with him. It could explode in her face. But if she sampled, he'd have to up the stakes big time. She did a quick calculation. "That's not even two per cent of the purse."

"Name your cut." He circled her desk like an opponent in the ring, and she caught a whiff of his aftershave. Cool spice.

A rush of air filled her lungs, and she let it hurl out in a miniature tornado. "Half the take, no sex, and I'm gone right after the ceremony."

He eyed her like he was going for her jugular. "Sex is a non-negotiable item in this deal." A guffaw ripped from deep in his throat. "A real marriage is the backer's price."

Nina grasped the mug between her hands, gulped several mouthfuls of the now lukewarm coffee and plunked it back on the coaster. The black brew sloshed the sides of the cup, but didn't spill. She picked up a pencil and tapped it on the desktop. She hadn't worked for Cade Sloan without learning a thing or two about savvy —make that cutthroat—business wheeling and dealing. She cleared her throat. "Fifty percent, one night of s-s-se—"

"With me." He grinned, and from her vantage it looked like a leer.

She ignored the hit. "*After* the ring's on my finger, one night with y-y-ou, and then I'm gone."

"*Hasta la vista*, babe?" He winked.

She nodded. She couldn't speak. Her heart squeezed itself into a fist. She must be nuts to engage in this deal with him. She had to find another way to fund her search…support her mother, herself, pay the PI, get answers, find her father.

"Works for me." He rolled up his sleeves and flexed his arms.

"It does?" She let herself consider her future husband-to-be. He was well built and tanned…must be all that trekking around constructions sites. The August heat branded his brown hair with sunlight, and she wondered how soft—

She paled in comparison, being cooped indoors with the air conditioning. Add to that her frumpy clothes, chunky shoes, eyeglasses and a hairstyle that'd gone out with the wagon train, and no one would give her a second look.

A quiver of a smile brushed her mouth. Beneath her outer garments, lace and silk sheathed her curves, but that was her secret. And that's how she liked it, how she planned it.

"Mmm," Cade murmured, a predator cornering his prey. No sweat with this deal. He'd charm the money from her, which was technically his anyway, and then unload her.

Cade dismissed the stab of his conscience.

For her trouble, she'd be tripping along with pocketfuls of cash as per his original offer. A slight easing around his heart. She'd collect on the rings too. She'd be set to go.

You schmuck. He shrugged. He'd been called worse.

"No regrets?" he asked, wondering why he bothered to voice the query.

"I'll let you know." She toyed with the pencil between her fingers, not meeting his eyes.

Chuckling, he bridged the distance between them and set his coffee mug next to hers. He was back on the playing field. Rebuilding the company would save hundreds of jobs and create new ones on the home front and overseas. He had nothing to feel guilty about, did he?

He loomed over her, so close he could smell her perfume—exotic blossoms of some kind. It knocked his senses into gear. "Take a memo, Ms. McLowsky."

She adjusted her eyeglasses and risked a peek at him from above the lenses.

He flashed her a wolfish smile. "Our merger goes into effect tomorrow."

CHAPTER TWO

"Tomorrow?" Nina plunked her hands on the computer keys, short-circuiting the flow of power and filling the screen with gibberish.

"Yep." Cade grunted, holding her hostage with his gaze.

Nina tapped the delete button and cleared the monitor, thankful that he didn't get a visual of the screen. She sighed, relieved, before a sliver of fear pierced her. She didn't like that look in his eye. She should have known it by now; that cunning, 'take no prisoners' mentality that had launched him into the mega millions bracket virtually overnight crossed over into his personal life. And now he had ensnared her.

He could get any woman he wanted, why choose her?

And why had she consented?

Couldn't she just delete the foolish agreement she made with her boss? Surely he wouldn't hold her to it. All she had to do was rescind—

"Not having second thoughts already?" he asked, his tone a challenge.

She jutted her chin and shook her head, her fingers poised over the keyboard. "You?"

Cade chuckled. "Not a chance."

He had to concede to his uncle's terms, even if it felt like a crowbar in his chest. If he didn't play along, the international bankers would hammer locks onto his businesses. With barely enough to cut expenses next month, he'd be shoveling gravel himself at the luxury condo development in Westchester.

The idea soured in his stomach.

The sudden clanging of an alarm clock wrenched him from his dark thoughts, and he scowled at his intended.

"Oops, sorry." Nina slapped the clock quiet, and didn't even bother looking his way. "I use the timer to pace my page count."

"Carry on." He circled her desk.

Cade had built his company into the billion dollar global economic force it was today virtually with his bare hands and a knack of hitting the bull's-eye on a construction deal. To have his life's work on the edge of destruction scoured his insides and pumped him into battle.

A distressing noise invaded his thoughts, and he refocused on Nina, slamming her coffee mug on the desk and muffling a cough with her hand.

"We-ent down the wrong way," she wheezed, reaching for a Kleenex.

"You want some water?" He patted her back and when a crackle of electricity singed his fingers, he pulled away. Static from her dress, he concluded, but the sensation shot into his arm and spread through him.

Hot. Arousing.

He frowned. Unusual.

"No-o." She shook her head, and a curl fell over her brow. "I'm fine, thanks." A flick of her fingers, and she smoothed it back in place.

"Are you always so efficient?"

"Excuse me?" she murmured, her attention on the computer screen.

"Nothing," he muttered, stepping away from her.

All this week until dawn today, he'd racked his brains for another solution to his dilemma. But this morning, he'd rolled out of bed, his pajama bottoms riding low on his hips and, scrubbing his unshaven jaw raw, trudged barefoot to the kitchen of his Park Avenue penthouse, while his lack of options mocked him. Seizing the percolator from the counter, he splashed stale coffee in a mug and taken a swig in hope of reviving his senses. Scratching his chest, he slogged to the living room, and sank on the sofa, the mug warming his palms.

A gamble in Monte Carlo or Las Vegas might dig him out if lady luck was on his side. A dim memory of his father turning a card at the gaming tables and online casinos surfaced. Cade took a gulp of the brew and the bitter taste grated his tongue. On a winning streak, William Sloan had strutted; but on a losing spiral—

Cade hauled himself up and walked to the wall of window, squinting at the sun rising over the Manhattan skyline, his eyes stinging from his sleepless night. Out in New York Harbor, shrouded by early morning mist he could see Lady Liberty standing strong and sure. A wry twist cracked his mouth. A toss of the dice was too risky…a fool's folly. He needed a sure hit.

A rumble erupted from deep in his chest, and he dumped half the coffee down his throat. In the distance a foghorn sounded, signaling it was time to get his butt to the office and face his creditors…and his secretary. Still he hesitated. He could sell out and liquidate his assets or refinance and cash out. But with real estate shifting from a sellers' to a buyers' market, he'd still be short by three million.

How had his uncle known the exact amount?

"Oh darn." The muffled exclamation and the scraping of a chair across the floor zoomed him back to the frontlines…and to her. Ms. McLowsky had already pulled out the mangled document from the printer, inserted new paper and resumed her stiff pose at the computer.

He skimmed her head, barely noticing the highlights glinting on her hair from the sunbeam filtering through the windowpane. His gaze bounced off the graceful line of her neck to her mouth, now pursed in concentration, her fingers tapping the keys. He had to buy himself some time, even if it meant being forced to the altar with...her.

The growl in his throat sounded, and Nina snapped her head up, her huge eyes mirrored through the lenses.

A pinprick to his heart, but he set his jaw and steeled every muscle in his body.

Collateral damage.

He was engaging in a battle on the global economic field to recoup his losses—little Nina McLowsky was simply collateral damage. He grunted.

"Is that part of the memo, sir?"

Snooty Ms. McLowsky? Well, well... he curved his mouth in a bemused smile. Might turn out to be the best fun he'd had in a long time.

"Very funny, Ms. McLows...er...Nina." Her name skimmed across his tongue like Southern Comfort, smooth, hot, sensuous. "Let's dispense with formality, shall we?" He loosened his tie. "Since we're about to tie the knot." He clicked his tongue. "For better or worse."

"Worse is what I'm thinking," she mumbled beneath her breath.

"What was that, Ms....er...Nina?"

******

Nina sat strapped in the seat of Century Corp's private Lear plane beside her husband and stared out the window at rain battering the runway. The summer storm had turned the day dismal, reflecting her thoughts. She twisted the gold band around her finger. Three hours. She'd been married to Cade Sloan all of three hours, and now about to jet across the globe for their honeymoon. She curled her fingers so tightly, her pink tipped nails bit into her palm. Moisture beaded her upper lip.

She glanced at him, slouched in his seat and snoozing like he hadn't a care in the world.

Her temples throbbed.

When the plane taxied down the runway of John F. Kennedy International Airport, she clutched the seat arms and held her breath.

Her insides shifted.

The aircraft picked up speed and then they were airborne.

A sigh of relief forced its way from her tight throat, and she unclenched her hands. She lifted a stray curl off her moist brow, patted the dampness with a tissue from her purse, and crumpled it between her fingers.

Her stomach rolled.

Gulping down nausea, she leaned her head to the side and shut her eyes, but that made it worse. She opened her eyes wide and collided with the intensity of his gaze. It socked her breast, shot into her heart and scrambled her vitals. She sucked in oxygen, desperately, and he bolted upright.

"You okay?"

She nodded, and then shook her head, her hand flying to her mouth.

"Here, lie back." He reclined the chair, placed his hand on her shoulder and eased her down. When he stretched across to adjust the light blanket over her, he accidentally bumped her breasts, sending an electrical sizzle into her.

She held her breath. He expelled his.

The subtle mint of his breath brushed her hot cheek, alerting her senses. He stayed near for another second. It seemed endless. Her pulse skyrocketed.

Thankfully, that took her mind off the tornado in her stomach.

Then he pulled away.

Pent up air in her lungs shot forth.

"Want something to eat?"

"Ummm," she mouthed, glaring at him.

"Bad choice of words, huh?" He curved his mouth in a half grin, a gesture that had her breath looping around her ribs. "Some water?"

She rolled her eyes.

"Guess not."

Heck, Cade didn't know what to do with a tipsy woman in the confines of the aircraft cabin. He squinted at Nina, and her pallor had him wanting to gather her into his arms and stroke her, to smell her subtle scent that seemed to wrap around his heart and not let go. He chuckled at his foolish musing. *Get a handle, Sloan.*

She'd do for a bit of wedding night bliss to seal the deal with the backer…then he'd keep his distance; avoid complications until such time as he could reasonably unload her.

"Shouldn't imbibe on booze on an empty stomach," he bit out. She must have overdone it with the pre-flight cocktails while he dozed; something he rarely did, but on his own cruiser, he felt he could steal a few moments of shut-eye.

She opened her mouth to give him some sass but quickly shut it tight.

"You'll feel better by the time we get to Larnaca." He set his jaw, knowing full well he had to go through the farce and show up there with his bride before collecting the cash.

Someone had set him up to take the fall. The sharks that he sicced on the case had clued the tip-offs came from an undisclosed location in Europe. In the meantime, he had to stack his arsenal to ensure a victory.

Cade glanced her way, and then retreated.

It'd work for him…a combo deal; business and pleasure.

He'd make sure of it.

He tossed her another look, and got booted somewhere in the vicinity of his heart for his trouble. Odd. Definitely odd. He waggled his shoulders and dismissed the feeling.

The one night with her should zip by without a hitch, and then he'd be off with Century Corp intact, pockets full and little Nina would be history.

"So, lie back and enjoy the ride Mrs…uh…Sloan," he muttered, doing the same.

******

The sun had turned the horizon into a blaze of color, and the Mediterranean Sea into liquid gold.

"Hungry?" Cade asked, just as his cell beeped.

Nina gave him a wan smile and a wave of her hand, but by then, he had stepped onto the balcony. That suited her fine, giving her some breathing space to rest up and regroup. She wobbled on her feet and eyed the bed before her gaze skittered to him now in earnest conversation. She opted for the couch. Tossing her purse on one end, she kicked off her sandals and collapsed on the cushions.

A sea breeze sailed towards her from the half open balcony doors.

It was balmy, sensual and soothing.

"You can use the bathroom first," Cade mouthed over the cell's mouthpiece.

She shook her head. A big mistake. The vibrations shot to her toes and back up to her belly, making her stomach heave. She closed her eyes.

Nina had endured the remainder of the flight, and had actually snoozed for a couple of hours while they flew over the Atlantic Ocean. Then before she realized it, they were descending over the Mediterranean, and toward the seaside Larnaca International Airport on the island of Cyprus. The jolt of the jet's wheels on the landing strip jostled her awake, and by the time she reoriented herself, they were disembarking.

A blast of heat smacked her face, and she stepped back, bumping into her husband's iron-hard chest. He took her elbow to guide her down the stairs, and shivers shot up her arm. She faltered in her step, and the strap of her sandal snapped loose.

"Steady there." He spanned her waist, his touch an electric charge to her nervous system, and lifted her over the last three steps of the aircraft's ladder. Just before he set her on her feet,

16

his temple brushed hers, and she glanced up, so close, she could see the brown tint of his lashes, smell— He glanced down, and she tumbled into his golden-brown gaze.

She held her breath, her heart pounding.

He shuttered his eyes, and let her go. "Okay now?"

"Mmm." She stepped onto the tarmac and mindless of the heat penetrating the soles of her shoes, gazed at the priceless view of ocean and sky. Salt tang in the air tickled her nose. A lone seagull squawked, and she lifted her head, the evening sun still bright enough to make her squint. She heard Cade's intake of breath as he filled his lungs with sea air, then grew quiet. Just for a moment, she allowed herself to imagine this was real, that she and Cade—

The surf crashed upon the rocks, shattering her fantasy and the fragile connection between them.

"Come on." He grabbed her wrist, dragging her through Customs, luggage claim and then to the limousine waiting outside the airport.

She'd managed the limo ride to Century Blue, one of his ocean front properties in Ayia Nappa, the playground of Western Europe, and the elevator ascent to the penthouse bridal suite. But by the time the bellman deposited their luggage in the foyer, accepted the generous tip from Cade and made his exit, she was a frazzled heap of nerves.

Felt it, and for sure must look it. What with her cotton shift wrinkled, her sandal flopping and her mussed hair sticking to her temples.

She flung an arm across her eyes, trying to forget her lack luster appearance—hardly the look of a glowing bride. Digging her toes beneath the cushions, she gulped down the whimper vibrating in her throat.

When Cade had shut the door behind the bellman, she started to panic. Would he pounce? Would she let him? After all, she made a bargain…a high-end deal with the mogul of Manhattan.

A hysterical sound bubbled in her chest and burst from her mouth in a muffled sound. Relief flooded through her when the cell call had cornered his attention.

She heard him pacing, his words floating to her on the evening breeze and disintegrating her thoughts.

"I got her." A muted chuckle. "By nightfall, she'll be docked, tied and ready to ride—"

A pause.

"She's not for sale yet."

In the background, waves pounded the beach, a crescendo of sound in a second of stillness.

"I've got dibs on her maiden voyage—"

From the courtyard down below, the *Bouzouki* musicians tuned up for the evening entertainment, and mouthwatering aromas of *souvlaki* cooked over an open grill wafted to her. She grabbed her middle; she for one would not be dining under the stars tonight.

The distraction eclipsed his words, and she crinkled her brow, trying to make sense of what she heard.

"A costly investment, I'll be paying—"

Her eyes flew open wide. *Me?*

The fluttering of curtain allowed her glimpses of the million-dollar ocean view, but her attention was glued on her husband.

"After I break her in, you can have her—"

"How dare you—" Nina made to jump up, jostled her insides, and fell back, closing her eyes, and pressing her mouth tight. She would not be sick. Would not be sick. Not now. Not in front of him.

"—if the price is right."

Sweat poured from her pores, soaking her wrinkled cotton dress…her wedding dress. What had she gotten herself entangled in?

"I'll sell—"

Sell her?

"—to the highest bidder."

She began to pant, then a whiz of sound fizzed between her teeth, and she lifted her lashes a fraction, snaring him in her focus.

Tall, dark and gorgeous…deceptive—dangerous.

Worse than she imagined. Yet, he looked so calm and cool, fresh in his white open necked shirt and denims he wore for their 'I do's' compared to her—a ragged mass of guilt ridden nerves. He whisked her off so quickly after the ceremony at New York City Hall, she'd had no time to change, her one travel bag already in the trunk of the Bentley.

"By midnight she'll be purring beneath my hands."

His words iced her skin.

Something was wrong; something very uncool, but she was too zoned out from the intercontinental flight, the emotional see-saw of the wedding—not what a girl dreamed of—the heat, and her queasy stomach, to figure it out.

"Yeah, I can handle her." A guffaw. "Should be an easy ride."

Nina seethed, a flush on her skin making her temperature rise and her ire about to explode.

"Naa."

An ominous silence.

"If you're willing to pay, she'll play—"

A chuckle.

It sent shivers crawling up her spine.

"I'll guarantee she'll be a real fine piece of a—"

Nina's hand flew to her throat, the other to her abdomen, her heart hammering. Dear God, what had she done? This was a snow job on her by none other than the king of con. She'd fallen for his duplicity and been fool enough to marry him. She cringed, gulping down bile rising in her throat. The acid taste curdled her stomach, and she tottered to her feet, weaving her way to the bathroom.

"Hey, you alright?"

The sounds from within must have alerted him, for he was there, knocking on the half open door. And her, with her head half in the toilet.

If the floor caved in and carried her out to sea, she'd be ever so grateful.

No such luck.

He loomed over her, a slight shift of his sneakers visible from her peripheral vision. Could it be that Mr. High and Mighty Sloan was uneasy about something? That gave her a lift, but it was short lived as another wave of nausea assaulted. She waved him back with her outstretched hand. He deserved a tongue-lashing, which she couldn't give in her present position. She heard the sink faucet running then—

"Here." He handed her a damp washcloth.

She mumbled her thanks and waved him out. "Go."

Cade squinted at her bent-over figure, zeroing in on her shapely tush outlined beneath the cotton material of her dress stretched taut and riding high on her slender thighs. A beauty mark teased. He paused, and then made his exit. "Be right here if you want—"

She extended a leg and booted the door shut in his face.

The toilet flushed.

Ten minutes later, Nina stepped from the bath and shrieked, trying to cover her naked body with her hands. "What are you doing here?"

"Come 'ere." Cade held open a towel for her, his voice sounding gruffer than he intended. "Don't want you catching cold."

"Concern for me?" She snatched the towel from his hand and wrapped it around herself.

She must be feeling better, he mused, plunking down on the toilet lid.

"You're an expensive investment." There, that'd get the ball back in his court pronto. Couldn't afford to be going soft on her. Better she thought him the s.o.b. the media pegged him. He curled his mouth in distaste…in the end he'd appear to be exactly that, maybe even worse, in her eyes. He shrugged, reminding himself; collateral damage.

She laughed, a dry sound that annoyed the heck outta him. He couldn't figure out why, and Cade Sloan always had answers.

She squinted up at him. "Which you haven't paid for yet." She swept her glasses from the sink ledge and propped them on her nose.

"After I've sampled the goods—" He paused, allowing his words to tell their own story. "We'll cash out in the morning." He wiggled his brows. "Divvy up the loot." He inclined his head toward a manila envelope on the coffee table, barely visible from her vantage point. "Wedding gift." His words crackled with cynicism. "Delivered when you were in the shower. The other half will arrive tomorrow."

"Your half or mine?"

"Very funny."

She fluttered her eyelashes and, about to smack him with a smart retort, she keeled over. He leaped up and caught her in his arms. For a heartbeat, she struggled against him, and then eased in his embrace. She smelled fresh…of soap, shampoo and woman. Different than most women whose heavy perfumes nearly knocked him out. A chuckle threatened, and he locked it in his throat. He scooped her up and took her to bed.

As soon as her head hit the pillow, she conked out. He allowed his gaze to travel from the damp hair framing her face to her smooth shoulders, pausing at her cleavage barely visible above the towel still wrapped around her body. Skimming her thighs, he noted the slight bend to her legs on the bedding, the curve of her calf, her slim ankles, the arch of her foot, her hot pink polished toenails. She had one arm sprawled over her head and the other bent, her hand cushioning her cheek. Her golden tipped lashes brushed her cheeks and the sprinkle of freckles on her nose made his lips twitch a smile. It vanished when he focused on her mouth. Palest pink. He could imagine it tasting sweet.

He shook his head. A sex kitten if he ever saw one. And he'd seen plenty. Logistically, with his work schedule it'd been impossible to do more than enjoy the view. A heavy sigh shoved its way from his belly, and he scratched his chin with his knuckles. He had his morals…and his instincts.

He could smell a bad rap a mile off. Made it a rule to stay clear of women who showed their claws, became too possessive and made demands—who would want to change him, complicating his life.

And for that, the newshounds coined him a callous 'love 'em 'n leave'em, s.o.b.'

A hollow sound burst from deep inside him.

Nina stirred, a moan almost a purr feathered from her lips.

He snapped out of his turbulent thoughts and focused on her. If she stayed wrapped up in that damp towel, she'd catch a cold. Gently, he removed her glasses and set them on the bedside table. Unfurling the towel from around her body, he got the breath knocked out of him. He sucked in a shot of air, burning his throat before filling his lungs. A heavy beat, and he exhaled, a sizzle of sound between his teeth. He pulled the covers over her body, touched her cheek in a fleeting caress and stepped away.

He wouldn't be sampling his high priced 'investment' tonight.

A series of chills grazed his nape, but he dismissed them as the effect of the night breeze drifting in from the balcony. He rubbed the back of his neck, and chuckled at his foolishness, his gaze fixed on the ugly duckling turned swan in his bed.

His jaw tightened, and he felt himself harden.

He drew in a deep breath, then another, before heading for the shower.

Tomorrow night. He'd bring this deal to a close.

CHAPTER THREE

It had taken Cade Sloan a year to the day to track down his gold-digging ex-spouse. Lil' Nina McLowsky had conned the con. He slid his powerful length from the limo and dismissed his chauffeur's attempt to open the door for him with a curt hand. He grimaced. Technically, she wasn't quite his ex yet, but she'd be soon enough. Right after he collected his dues.

"Meet me here in one hour." He glanced at the hot pink *Fantasy Secrets* sign splashed above the boutique's entrance and curled his lip in a silent snarl.

"*Si, Signore* Sloan." The chauffeur tipped his hat, sat back in the driver's seat, drove past the Fountain of Neptune next to the *Palazzo Vecchio*, and eased his way toward *Via Cassio*; the limo appearing out of place amidst the *Vespas*, a popular mode of transport for the Florentine locals.

Cade turned to bridge the two steps to the storefront, when the door swung open, giving him a view of the shapely backside of a blonde.

A muscle jarred his jaw.

It was her. Even with hair several shades lighter, he'd know her anywhere.

"*Mille grazie*, Julie for locking up today." She propped a pair of sunglasses on her crown, whirled around, her shoulder handbag swinging, and smacked into him.

"Steady there," he muttered, grabbing her shoulders. Heat sizzled through his shirt…her flame…and straight into his heart, but the padlock of ice made it fizzle to a vapor. Nonetheless, the impact left a bruise in the proximity of said organ, but he barely felt it…it had grown a scab.

"Oops, *mi scusi*—" She glanced up and color drained from her face. She swayed on her stiletto heels and his hands tightened over her arms. "You?"

"Me." The one word shot from his mouth like a bullet in the air between them.

Her coke bottle-thick glasses had disappeared. Her lashes heavy laden with mascara framed her baby blues, now on alert. Her pink-painted mouth unsmiling. He shifted his gaze lower and got a boot in the groin. Her summer dress molded her every curve—the swell of her breasts, the accent of her waist, the roundness of her hips. Her legs were bare, tanned, sexy. He smothered a grunt. Her hair tied back with a pink ribbon, flowed down her shoulders, and he remembered how silky— No. He didn't want to go there. Strictly out of bounds.

"We're closed." Nina pushed him aside, her gold hoop earrings jangling, and moved one step up to gain the extra height to look him in the eye. At five foot two, every inch counted. What she glimpsed in his golden-brown gaze knocked her back and she seized the doorjamb for support. Her pulse pounded, and she licked her lips.

He zeroed in on her mouth, and his Adam's apple moved. A long, hot beat, and he shrugged.

"Haven't come for your…er…services—"

The crack of her hand across his cheek made her palm vibrate, but he barely flinched, except to shackle her wrist between his iron hard fingers.

"I've come for you." He coiled his lip in a near sneer. "To collect a debt owed."

"We're history." She lowered her Roberto Cavalli sunglasses over her eyes and made to go past him.

"Right after you pay up, lil' darlin'."

"I owe you nothing."

He yanked her slam hard against his chest, swooped down and stole a kiss. "That's a hint of what you owe, in addition to the million and a half you slipped out with." Deliberately, he removed her sunglasses and hooked them in the pocket of his shirt.

She went to snatch them back, and he leaned away from her reach.

"Uh, uh." He clicked his tongue. "Must've cost a euro or two, mmm?"

Oh, but he was a horrible man. How could she have imagined she'd felt anything for him but loathing—her eyes strayed to the smattering of hair on his chest visible by his half unbuttoned shirt, and excitement grazed the fury sizzling through her. Must be the shock of seeing him again, she reasoned.

"You were going to double cross me," she accused, shoving him back. He allowed a small space between them, but still anchored her hand with his.

He arched a thick brow. "Really."

"I heard you plotting—" her voice broke and she turned away.

"And so you decided to double deal me first."

Good gosh, he hadn't even denied it. She blew a stray hair from her eye, batted an eyelash and hoped her contact lens stayed in place. Perspiration glazed her skin and made her mini dress stick to her thighs. Her heart flipped and her stomach flopped. She had to get away from him quickly.

"This is insane." She spun around and faced him. "You paid me to marry you. I did. Now we're done."

"Sure thing, babe." He rubbed the gold circle at his earlobe with his thumb and index finger. "Right after you deliver on your promises." He laughed, a hollow sound that seemed to ricochet off the terracotta roofs of the neighborhood. "Som'm 'bout to love, honor—"

"I don't owe you—"

He tilted the corner of his mouth in a smirk. "—and obey."

She gaped at him in disbelief, and then blinked a rapid tempo. "I upheld my end of the bargain."

"Hardly." Cade released her hand, and shoved his in the pocket of his Armani pants, the empty feeling in his gut rankling. "You skipped out on me from the hotel in Ayia Napa before I cracked an eye open in the a.m."

She gulped, and he noted the motion. He liked that and, about to cut to the chase, he paused. Her features had a pinched look about them, even though it was August, and in Florence, Italy, that came with a heat wave. He must be having this effect on her. Good. He felt a jab of his conscience, but he ignored the warning.

"What do you want?" she demanded.

"Now there's a loaded question."

Her eyes flashed blue flame. "I'm not going to play your game." She took a step to walk by him, and he sidestepped her, blocking her path.

"Nor I yours, madam."

"Don't call me that," she snapped. "I married you and—"

Church bells rang from the *Campanile* of *The Duomo* in the heart of the city, slightly off cue, but filled the air with a sweet sound.

"And?"

"And nothing," she murmured.

"Exactly."

A sigh struggled from deep inside her. "What is it you want, Cade?"

"You."

She started, and her hand fluttered to her throat. "No." Shaking her head, she stepped away from him, and that only goaded him more.

"Yes." He advanced a step closer, and a wayward gust sent her subtle perfume his way. He balled his other hand behind his back and allowed the sensual feel to wash over him. Long ago, he promised himself to never let a woman, any woman get under his skin, and he'd done just fine until Ms. Straitlaced here landed in his life. A mirthless snort sounded from him. "And the loot you pilfered from under my nose."

Her betrayal had hit a raw nerve…it nicked him more than he realized. He hadn't tried to analyze why, but she'd done exactly what his mother had done, hadn't she?

Ditched him.

At first, he debated whether to write Nina off as a bad business investment and cut his losses, or pursue to recover all. But when an unidentified source hinted his espoused might be connected in some way with his business losses, it had him crunching nails between his molars. He was getting close to nabbing the perpetrator, but first, he had to know the truth about her.

The speed of the marriage had left a prenup in limbo, and she'd used it to her advantage. He pursed his mouth, shaking his head. When she had skipped out with the cash the day after their wedding, she slashed him right in the jugular of his company's financial hemorrhage.

She gutted his insides.

The thought scorched his mind and broiled his tongue.

"You will return every penny." Ahh, revenge was sweet. "Plus interest."

Nobody made a fool of Cade Sloan and got away with it. And certainly not one lil' Nina McLowsky…Sloan. He'd had to do some quick talking when he hadn't produced the bride, but the marriage license had given him a grace period to unveil her to the backer. Having just grazed by from the financial cyclone that had nearly whipped him into the dust, he was pumped to get the guy, but first he'd deal with her. Would she inadvertently lead him to the hacker?

"I don't have that kind of money."

"Too bad." His words were chips of ice.

"I-I-I sunk it all in my business and—"

"Yes?"

"Nothing."

"I'm not an unreasonable man—"

She snorted, but somehow on her it came out sexy. Something that only aggravated him more.

"I suggest you think of an ulterior payment plan then."

Her head snapped up, her eyes wide, suspicious. "Or?"

He shrugged, nonchalant. "You must've heard that this block adjacent to the *Piazzale Michelangelo* is due for demolition—"

"I was just on my way to the city—" Then, it dawned on her, and she paled. "You're the one gouging this historic…"

"Condo development, rezoning, modern trends in architecture—"

"All for a buck—"

"Something you like plenty of."

She glared at him, her lashes fluttering and betraying her inner angst.

"You care nothing about destroying people's lives, livelihoods, landmarks—"

The Vasari Corridor connecting the Palazzo Medici to the Palazzo Vecchio, the shops on stilts by the River Arno, the Uffizi & Academia museums boasting Michelangelo's, Leonardo Di Vinci's and Botticelli's masterpieces flashed through her mind. "You're an insensitive boor."

Her dart zinged his heart, but he toughened his jaw, appearing exactly as she coined him. "If I don't do it, someone else will."

"And that makes it alright?"

"Right?" he bit out. "You're talking to me about what's right and wrong?"

"I won't let you do it."

He chuckled. "I don't see how you're going to stop me." A telling pause. "Unless—"

Nina squirmed, feeling like she'd been blasted back a year…back into the clutches of one Cade Sloan, the playboy of Manhattan.

Except this was Florence, Italy, her turf; but even with her Italian designer shoes and haute couture armor, he still rattled her.

A sigh shot from deep inside her, and for a moment she got lost in her thoughts. In the year she'd been here, the city had welcomed her and in no time, she felt at home and part of the community. She'd been enchanted by the city and its people, their culture and their history.

The palazzos, basilicas, museums—a smile quivered on her lips—and the famous Florentine Café Giubbe Rossi in the Piazza della Repubblica where she strolled to get her mocha cappuccino, viewing the luxury brands of fashion, footwear, handbags, fragrances of Salvatore Ferragamo, Gucci, Prada, Chanel—all an inspiration to build her business.

Starting a new life in the City of Gold had been both scary and exciting, but for once Nina had felt like she had control of her life.

"Unless, what?" she spit back, the Amazon rising inside her.

Here, she thought she'd be so far from his sphere, he'd not give her a second thought, let alone trek after her. She squinted up at him. Well, she wouldn't let one Cade Sloan bulldoze what she worked so hard to build. She'd battle it out with him. And if she got some cuts and bruises in the process—her hand flew to her heart—the brunt of the injury would be there.

"Unless you're willing to negotiate," he said, dangling a carrot. "And even with that" –he delivered his shot— "there's no guarantee the sledgehammer won't divert and land smack center on your boutique."

A groan ripped from her mouth before she could bite it back. "You're a controlling bast—"

"You've developed quite an opinion of me over the year." He smirked. "Or had you always thought of me in x-rated terms?"

"Go take a hike, Sloan."

"You better pack up your inventory then." He took out his cell and keyed in the number. "The van will be here tomorrow a.m. to move you out" –he paused— "how's it go…uh…yeah… lock, stock and bar—"

"What're you doing?" she demanded, and on reflex grabbed his forearm. His muscles contracted beneath her fingers, hard, strong, unyielding.

He cocked a brow, and glanced down at her hand curled over his arm.

Instantly she let go, but by then it was too late. Sexual energy vibrated between them, heating up the atmosphere to near combustion. The tension mounted. She stumbled back a step and slammed up against the shop window.

"Taking care of business." Someone must have answered for he spoke into the mouthpiece. "Reschedule the demolition for day after tomorrow."

"Wait." A bare whisper, but he heard.

A pause. "I'll get back to you on that." He clicked off the cell and skewered her with his dark gaze.

"I-I'll pay you i-in installments." She hated contemplating a deal with him, but she'd find a way, she'd manage somehow. She would. And then she'd put a million miles between Cade Sloan and herself. She gulped. She thought she'd done that a year ago, and here he was on her doorstep, catapulting her back into his life.

"Sure thing."

"You-you're agreeing?"

"Mmm," he mouthed. "But it'll be on my schedule and my call."

"What's that supposed to mean?"

"Pack your bags, Mrs. Sloan," he said, a glint in his eye and a wolfish slant to his mouth. "You're coming with me to the top of Troodos Mountains in central Cyprus."

"W-why there?"

"Because it suits me."

She swayed, and he placed his hand on her shoulder to steady her. She flinched. But not fast enough. High voltage charged into her, sending her nerves on a sensual spin.

"Not another upset stomach, I hope." He angled his head, and she didn't miss the underlining reference to their wedding night when she spent most of it bent over the toilet bowl. "Much too convenient…and suspicious, wouldn't you say?"

"Outline your terms, Sloan." She straightened her shoulders, her tone all business.

"Oh, I intend to."

"The sooner this is over with the better."

His eyes darkened. Hers sparked with indignation.

A tension-filled moment staggered by.

"You will resume your position as my—"

"Wife," she murmured, the barely audible word an accusation.

"Hardly," he countered.

Her head shot up.

His brows bunched, shielding his gaze.

"As my secretary cum housekeeper cum bedmate."

His words were like frost bite on her already raw emotions. Humiliating. She nearly passed out, but a mouthful of air filled her lungs and steadied her.

"And whatever else I please to have you …perform." His savage tone ripped her flesh, and more so her heart bled.

She wouldn't do it. Couldn't.

"Never." She fired back, her pride kicking in.

His eyes glittered an ice storm, and he shrugged. "Start boxing your merchandise. You don't want to lose that along with the building." He towered over her, watching her like a hawk and noting every nuance of emotion cross her face.

This had to do more than with her business. Her decision would impact not only her life, but those she cared for, including this quaint city she now called home.

Home. How sweet that sounded.

But not with Cade Sloan.

She fingered the chain around her neck, and was sure he caught the contempt reflected in her body language, the twist of her mouth and the glint in her eyes, by the narrowing of his own.

Her wedding ring nestled between her breasts, just barely hidden from his view by the neckline of her dress. She didn't normally wear clothes that were this risqué, but during work hours she had an image to uphold…good for business and so she had fun with fashion trends. As for the ring, she kept it as a reminder of her folly, and something else she didn't want to identify. Right now, she felt like yanking if off and hurling it in his face, but thought better of it.

The lion was already riled, and she didn't want to add fuel to his fury quite just yet. Could she beat Cade Sloan at his own game?

He stepped down and was about to turn away.

She took a step after him, and then stopped. She'd be selling herself to him. Something seemed to wither and die inside her. If she didn't agree to his terms, her mother would suffer…would have no life at all. Her assistant, Julie, who'd helped her selflessly this last year in the midst of a raging custody battle against her Greek husband, would be forced to rely on handouts to take care of herself and her baby. Nina inhaled, filling her lungs with much needed oxygen. Her mission to find her father impeded by Cade's arrival and demands.

Moisture dampened her nape, and she glanced toward one of the city's many Basilicas, praying she made the right choice. If she chose wrongly, others could be hurt by the backlash. Either way, destruction lay in her path, but the lesser of the two evils was Cade Sloan.

"Wai-t," she called, the word sounding like a croak, foreign even to her own ears.

He turned and sized her up from head to toe, sending a blush to coat her body.

She swallowed, fanning her face with her hand. Somewhere in the back of her mind—or was that her heart—a danger signal flared. Hadn't she cut a disastrous deal with this man before? She survived the first…could she do it a second time? She closed her eyes, and blackness undulated before her, then a shaft of light.

Perhaps through the rubble of her life, she could ensure a safe haven for her mother, who refused to budge from the familiar — her neighborhood, her church, her friends—and was still foolish enough to believe her husband would return to her. Nina twisted her mouth in a wry line, and then softened it to a trace of a smile. And she would be helping Julie and her child.

Oh, but she'd fight him every inch of the way. No man, especially Cade Sloan, would control or dictate to her, she reminded herself. Brave words, but she shriveled inside. *That's exactly what'll happen, girlie, if you agree to his terms.* Cornered, she had to play to his tune, at least for now. But she'd find a way to infiltrate a note or two of her own.

"For how long?" The question forced its way between her lips.

"As long as it takes." His ruthless words were like shards of metal imbedding beneath her skin. "And that'll depend on you."

"What'd you mean?" Her eyes narrowed, her pulse skipped.

He shot her a killer smile, sending both heat and chills up her spine.

"How well you perform your duties."

"Go to he—!"

"My local hangout?" He snared her shoulders with his hands and hauled her smack against his chest, his eyes smoldering. "You'll join me, won't you?"

CHAPTER FOUR

Nina heard the chopper, the sound out of sync with the turbulent atmosphere between Cade and herself in the confines of the shack he'd brought her to three weeks ago.

"Your coffee." She held the tray out to him with the bittersweet Greek brew in the demitasse and a glass of water, tempted to dump it over his head. Sighing, she swiped a stray strand off her brow, sure that a streak of soot smeared her cheek, and stared out the window.

On a clear day, she could catch a glimpse of Mount Olympus, the tallest peak of the Troodos Mountains. Tile-roofed homes dotted the mountainside amidst the pines, paved roads gave access to other parts of the island, while dirt paths led to the alpine village marketplace, and to the *kafeneon,* the café in the square; she had stumbled across it one day while shopping, and—she blinked moistness from her eyes, her pulse smashing against her ribs. She had to go talk with him…tell her mother. She gulped the emotion rising up to choke her.

"No thanks." Cade logged off his laptop and scribbled on a notepad without so much as a glance her way.

"I stood toiling over the hot—" She plunked the tray on the rough-hewn table, and placed her hands on her hips, the burlap sack dress she wore to annoy the heck outta him, chafed her skin, but she ignored the discomfort. "You said you wanted another cup."

"I changed my mind." He rubbed the crick in his neck, his gaze shielded. "But I do want a hearty breakfast, pronto."

"Yes, sir. Right away, sir."

"Don't call me sir," he barked.

"Yes, sir."

He set his pen down and slammed the notepad shut.

"Hmm." She eyed the basketful of eggs on the shelf, she'd chased the hens around the yard at the crack of dawn to collect. "Poached, over easy, sunny side—" She lifted a well-defined eyebrow, and grabbed a couple of eggs, sizing them up in her hands.

He caught her intention. "Hold on—" But he didn't stand a chance.

"Your breakfast, sir." She whirled first one and then the other at him. "Scrambled eggs, coming right up."

He ducked, and the yolks splattered the whitewashed dirt wall.

"Temper, temper." He gave her a lopsided grin, and knocked her pulse off rhythm. "Now see what you've done? Extra work for yourself."

His censuring tone made her hackles rise, and she stomped her foot on the dirt floor, her ire about to explode.

"Gotta move." Smart man that he was he caught his cue, pushed his chair back and stood, but his gaze roamed over her in her rags. For a split second, he held her gaze with his own, and then he turned away, booting the chair back in place.

Was he feeling guilty? Well, then good. He brought her to this archaic place to be at his beck and call, and she played her part of cinder girl to the hilt. She dressed the part, spoke the part, acted the part. She crinkled her brow. That may have turned him off, for except for ordering her around, he hadn't laid a hand on her. That should've pleased her, but instead, she bristled with irritation.

But then, her fighting spirit reared. He wanted a serving wench, and that's what he got. Except for her lacy undergarments, she refused to wear the trendy clothes she brought into this no man's land. She'd dumped potatoes from a sack, shook it clean, snip-snapped holes and pulled it over her head. The sacks came in a variety of colors—plenty to choose from.

"Be ready by eight tonight."

"What for?"

He stepped closer and his coffee laced breath warmed her cheek. She swallowed, but he merely flicked the rip flapping on the swell of her breast from the burlap barely reaching her thighs. His fingertips skimmed her flesh, sending tingles shimmying up her spine.

He paused, debated.

Her pulse skittered, and she gritted her teeth.

"Wear something more becoming."

He trailed his fingers down her soot-smeared arm and took her hand. An epithet shot from his mouth, abrading the atmosphere between them, and she curled her fingers, hiding her broken nails and raw fingertips.

"What have you done to your hands?" he growled. "I told you to wear gloves when you're working."

She yanked her hand away from his. "I'll do as I please, Sloan." The rubber gloves ripped too easily and it was faster to do the chores gloveless.

She lathered lotion on her hands and body, but the daily manual labor of fetching and carrying in the sun had taken its toll. On the plus side, she'd gotten a superb tan without the expense of a salon; her skin glowed with health and vitality, but he didn't notice. Hadn't cared to.

A storm brewed in his eyes. "Why do you wear that shapeless sack?"

She pointed her chin in defiance. "It's hardly fitting for a serving wench to dress up. Up at the crack of dawn, peeling potatoes, cooking, washing, feeding the chickens, dumping slop to the hogs—"

"Hogs?"

"Well, maybe not exactly." She focused over his head to avoid his incredulous gaze. "But the piggy will grow—"

He laughed. The man dared laugh. A deep-throated sound that ricocheted off the walls and sensitized every nerve in her body.

She rattled on to distract from that sensation. "Hauling jugs from the water pump and—"

"I told you not to do that." He scrubbed a hand across his cheek. "I'd take care of it."

"I'm not helpless." That of course, defeated her purpose in prattling off her servile duties. "Tend the garden, do the laundry, dishes—" She paused for breath, and for effect snatched up the broom from against the wall. "Sweep the floor, make the bed—"

"Ahh, the bed." He strolled over and bounced on the edge of the mattress, his gaze never leaving her face. "Sturdy enough for two."

A rooster crowed, the chickens clucked, and the noise of the chopper grew louder.

Impatience crossed his features at the untimely interruption. He leaped up, strode to the door and tossed over his shoulder. "Find something suitable for tonight."

"Excuse me?" She'd put up with this servitude, checking off her duties from the list he left each morning before flying to the worksite. For him to add another demand didn't go down too well. Not at all.

"Major upscale." He glanced at her feet, and feeling vulnerable, she curled her toes, the dirt floor rough beneath her soles. "And wear shoes."

She snapped up the rag from the table and hurled it at him.

He ducked, their eyes at a tug-of-war.

"If I don't?"

He tilted his mouth in that lazy smile that had her heart tripping. "I'll dress you myself."

Annoyance eclipsed the sizzle of excitement zipping through her at the image his words evoked. Why didn't she just walk, or stomp out and be done with it? The reason was obvious of course; he held all the cards… for now. "I have plans of my own."

His smile disappeared, and his eyes darkened.

"Cancel them." Cade caught the glitter of resentment in her eyes, heck practically every time she looked at him. A sliver of feeling nudged his heart, but he remained resolute. She'd not make a fool out of him again. To avoid the temptress, he knocked himself out readying a string of luxury floating hotels docked at Limassol Harbor, and about to sail the Greek Isles.

By the time he came home, Nina was already asleep; he got some shuteye on a stack of hay in the barn, which suited him for now. To touch her would melt the ice around his heart, and he couldn't allow that…not yet. Not until he found out her involvement in the scam.

Bunching his eyebrows, he studied her and got jabbed in the gut again. He tightened his abs, resisting the hit. Dressing in those dowdy threads didn't camouflage her lithe body and shapely curves…her derriere, her hips, her breasts… Savagely, he clamped down on the erotic images pummeling his brain, stalked to the table and seized his laptop and notes.

"You don't own me," she spat.

A smirk. "Until you pay up, I do."

"You can't keep me under lock and key."

"I can, but this is hardly a prison." He inclined his head toward the door and open windows of the one room shack, his gaze straying to the firepit and back to the rumpled bed where she slept. He crossed the floor, his peripheral vision gliding over her thighs, her knees, calves, slim ankles and dirt covered feet.

Another slam against his ribs.

Even with all that filth, she turned him on, and that irritated his male ego. To combat his lust, and he was sure that's all it was, cold showers in the outdoor stall iced his aroused flesh on a daily basis.

He tightened his jaw, and smacked down the rumble in his chest. He'd have her all right, but on his call and his time. His pulse thumped, and a warning bashed his brain, but he crunched it with his next words.

"Any more complaints?" he growled.

"Plenty."

"Save them."

He heard the chopper about to land, and yanked the door open, wanting nothing better than to scoop her up in his arms and stand with her beneath the spray. The scent of orange blossom in the air, and a hint of her exotic perfume spiked his ardor even with all that soot on her skin. Images of lathering her body, her hair, burying his face in her neck, her mass of tangled curls, tasting her, fondling—had him growing rock hard.

Breath sizzled between his teeth. Making out with his woman, his wife…could she ever really be his?

A silent snarl exploded inside him. *Don't be a fool, man.* Everything pointed to her in cahoots with the culprit who schemed to bring him down.

"Wear something classy." He paused on the threshold, his tone intimating he doubted she could do it.

"I'll wear what I please."

"Style." A look of warning, and he stepped outside, slamming the door behind him.

She wrenched the door open and marched after him, her lips a straight line, her eyes narrowed. "Why?" The word shot from her mouth like a knife between his shoulder blades.

"It's time to show off my three million dollar trophy."

"Ooh!" She hurled the broom at him, but it landed several yards short of his boots, and that frustrated her all the more.

A pulsing moment, and he swept up the broom and propped it against the water pump. "You'll need this for clean-up duty." He surfed her body with his narrowed gaze, and marched on. "You're quite inventive; your Boutique attests to that."

"If you've done anything to jeopardize—"

"What?" He paused in stride, his back a brick wall.

"Julie's been manning the shop since you and I—"

He spun around. "You and I—what?"

She ignored the verbal trap. "She needs the money for her baby—"

"Spare me the sob story…I've heard worse," he muttered, his words crackling with cynicism. "The one who cries often has more cash stashed than—" Isn't that what prompted him not to trust those who once, long ago, had been close to him? His mother, his father, and his uncle. At the age of six, Cade had been tossed to his uncle, while his parents jetted the globe. His uncle, the one who'd instigated this wager between Nina and him.

Cade had been betrayed by them all.

He grimaced. Intelligence pointed to the hacker being one of his circle. He glowered at Nina, standing in the path of a sunbeam, looking sexy as hell in her rags. Hadn't she struck out at him when he was down… almost down for the count?

He was in no mood to play good guy.

"You have no heart," she blurted.

That cut him deep.

"Eight. Class. Pull it off."

He sprinted to the chopper, his head slightly bent against the force of wind from the rotor and vaulted into the passenger seat. It was right on schedule to fly him to Paphos to oversee the multi-million-dollar redevelopment project he scooped from beneath his uncle's nose. Every time he aced his uncle from a prime real estate deal, he should've felt proud, but instead he felt detached.

The pilot engaged the controls; they were airborne and Cade glanced down. Nina snatched up a lemon from beneath the citrus tree and hurled it at the departing bird…er…him.

"I have a heart Mrs. Sloan, but it's out of bounds to you," he muttered, the words for his ears alone.

The pilot cast him a perplexed look.

Cade rubbed his knuckles across his chin to cover the awkward moment. "Can this bird fly any faster?"

CHAPTER FIVE

"Horrid man!" Nina stamped her foot, scooped up another lemon off the ground, aimed for the disappearing chopper, then changed her mind. She'd squeeze it, imagining it was Cade's neck, and soak her hands and feet in the juice. The citric acid would cleanse and whiten her nails. She cringed. Her tender fingertips would sting like heck, but she'd tough it out.

A sly smile tilted her mouth, and she tossed the lemon in the air and caught it in the palm of her hand.

Pull it off?!

He implied that she might not. Well, she'd do better than that. She'd shock the heck out of them all. Class on the cheap side should do it.

With a spring in her step, she headed for the house. Oh yes, she'd give them all something to gawk at, especially her espoused. But first, she'd make a quick trip to the village. She had walked the mile long path on several occasions since she had no transport. Cade had seen to that, although he left her a cell phone for emergencies. Imagine that, she smirked.

Thirty minutes later, Nina marched onward, the scent of pine filling the air, fresh, clean, invigorating. The early morning mist dissipated with the rising sun, warming her back, and she wished she were sunbathing on the sandy beaches of Ayia Napa. When she was out of Cade's clutches, she'd—

A jeep zoomed past, and she leaped to the side, nearly wrenching her ankle on the embankment. "Crazy driver," she muttered, and regaining her balance, hurried on.

******

Cade was inspecting the building site, when his cell beeped.

"Sloan." He booted a stone, and watched it hurl through the air and plunge into the depths with barely a splash.

Was that where he was headed? And was his wife the one booting him into the abyss?

He ignored the lacerations in his gut, his savage words a cover for his pounding pulse. "Apprehend her." He jogged to the chopper, signaled the pilot for take-off and barked orders into the mouthpiece. "Contain her at the house 'til I get there."

After twenty minutes, the whirlybird landed on the open turf and Cade leaped out, sprinting for the shack. His security stepped aside, and he burst through the front door. He slammed it shut behind him, and his eyes torpedoed Nina sitting on the bed, her chin defiant, her baby blues stormy.

"How dare you do this?" She leaped up and came swinging at him. "Having your men chase me in their jeep, spying on me—"

Cade sidestepped her blow, every sinew in his body taut, a mocking tilt to his mouth. "So, you *can* wear something else besides the sack."

Her short shorts showed off her tanned legs, the roundness of her tush. He blinked…was that a belly button ring glinting from beneath the crop top barely covering her breasts, rising and falling with her agitation? When had she pierced her navel, and who'd done the job? Who was she dressing up for? Like heck it wasn't him.

"What were you doing at the village plaza?" he snarled.

She shrugged, and that infuriated him more.

"A secret assignation with the bartender?" The words crackled white-hot between his clamped teeth.

"No!"

"Why were you exchanging money?"

"None of your business," she spat, and turned her back on him.

"Wanna bet?" He spun her around and seized her shoulders. She made to kick him.

He stepped beyond her reach and cocked a brow. "Nice sandals too." Then he jammed her hard against his chest, her heartbeat knocking his askance, her breath whizzing from her mouth teasing his nape.

It stoked the inferno inside him, and he lowered his head, crushing her mouth with his. She wiggled in his grasp, but as he deepened the kiss, she became pliant in his arms, kissing him back. Every muscle corded his torso, and he gathered her closer into the curve of his arm, his hand sliding around her midriff, his fingers dallying at the trinket on her navel, then higher, barely brushing her breasts on his way to cup her cheek.

Her intake of breath, a confirmation she wasn't immune to his touch … or to him.

He nipped her bottom lip, signaling he wanted entrance into her mouth. Bunching her hair in his hands, he held her head in place and readied for the sensual onslaught. She purred, a sexy sound, and wrapped her arms around his neck, giving him access. He licked…nibbled her lips, then slipped his tongue inside, tasting, stroking, waltzing with hers…a mating ritual… heaven.

Hell.

Taunts bombarded his brain, and he fought against the near combustion of their heat. Every pore in his body oozed sweat, and he could feel the dampness beneath her own clothes, her scent an erotic catalyst to his senses. He gripped her shoulders, his mouth fused with hers, still reluctant to pull away.

A knock on the door, and he blinked awake from the fantasy in his arms.

"One hour, Mr. Sloan." The security guard called from behind the closed partition.

Cade grunted his response, and with every fiber in his body resisting, he pulled away from her, his pulse booming at his temples, blood rushing to his male counterparts. He drew in a heavy breath and it fizzled between his gridlocked teeth. Battling the betraying thoughts, he stroked her cheek and cupped her chin in his palm, his thumb brushing her half-parted mouth.

"Cade?" she whispered, her eyes dark with passion.

Or was that deception?

When he didn't answer right away, she let her arms slide from his neck, and stepped back…a wobble of a step. "Is something wrong?"

He arched a brow. "You tell me."

"I don't know what you mean." She straightened her shoulders, standing strong, but fluttered her lashes, not quite meeting his eyes.

And that had a growl building inside him. What was she hiding?

The woman was a chameleon, and he had to unveil the real Nina Sloan before it was too late for her…him…them.

He pulled an envelope from the inside pocket of his jacket and hurled it at her feet, the contents spilling on the floor.

She blanched, and barely glanced at the photos, her hand fluttering to her throat, her eyes wide with alarm. "Why did you do this?" She raised her head, her glare bouncing off the icy sheen in his eyes. "Have me followed, have me restricted, have me—" Her voice cracked, and she swallowed the rest of her words.

"Who is he?" He trapped the photo of her with a man, his face hidden in the shade of a trellis of grapevines, beneath his boot. He wouldn't fall for her innocent deception, her ploys, her—

In a ruthless motion, he cemented his thoughts midstream, all but one. Everything pointed to her—the one who brought him down, now living under his roof. Nina Sloan. His insides blistered, then iced over at the possibility.

Nina, who moments ago sizzled with him in an erotic waltz of the senses. The image had every muscle in his body tensing, his pulse pumping at speed, her betrayal detonating his sphere.

"No one." She shook her head, and if it were possible, seemed to become a shade paler.

He seized her wrist and hauled her up against him, so close he could see the blue of her irises darken. Bitter taste scoured his tongue. "Answer the question."

"No."

He shuttered his eyes, his mouth a grim line. "No?"

She shoved him back and twisted away, rubbing her wrist.

He let her go, and regret rippled through him at the imprint of his fingers on her flesh. "Sorry, I didn't mean to hold on to you so hard."

Heck, he wanted to do more than hold onto her. He wanted to feel, touch, taste her—even now at the prospect she might be linked to the crackpot who'd stolen from him, he wanted her—wanted to—

He crushed the temptation by the power of his will, but his pulse pounded like a steel hammer. War raged between his heart and his mind... common sense. But there was no peace in sight until he knew the facts, the total truth about her.

Nina and the man in the photo.

She backed away and collapsed onto the cot, eyeing him with suspicion.

Cade nearly laughed out loud. She was the one under suspicion not him.

"If you won't talk now, you will certainly do so later."

"A threat, Cade?" She sprang to her feet, her body language a challenge.

"No threats, Nina." He curled his lip in derision. "Truth."

He allowed his gaze to drift over her; from her ponytail to her sandal encased feet, and then bounced back up, pausing at her cleavage. Her intake of breath was razor sharp in the confines of the room. He lifted his sights a tad higher, and smacked into her accusing eyes. But he persisted; each word an ice pellet shooting from his mouth.

"What were you doing at the *kafeneon*?"

She blew a stray hair off her face. "Having coffee." She nipped her bottom lip with her teeth.

His abs turned iron-hard. Her taste still lingered on his tongue, her perfume clinging to his shirt; his reaction to her sexually was nearing explosive levels. A muscle battered his jaw. He lowered his lids a fraction, studying her for any cue that his suspicions were unwarranted.

"You exchanged money."

She eyed him back, her voice overly sweet. "I paid for it."

"Nina…" Her name like sandpaper on his tongue abraded the air, the warning tone unmistakable.

"I had coffee, I paid for it," she snapped. "What do you want me to say, Cade?"

"The truth." He collided with the blue fire in her gaze.

"The truth?" Nina murmured almost to herself, then chuckled. "I went shopping."

"For?"

A smile curved her mouth, but didn't quite reach her eyes. "Why, for our dinner date, what else?"

"What else indeed." He rubbed his nape. This woman drove him to the brink. But he'd get the truth out of her one way or the other. "Well then, you'd better get dressed."

She kicked off her sandals and paused, her hand on the snap fastening of her shorts. "Are you going to watch?"

"Thirty minutes max," he growled, and stalked out.

CHAPTER SIX

"How ever did you land him, darling?" The woman raised her pencil-thin eyebrows and twisted her scarlet mouth in disdain. "Certainly not with your fashion sense."

Nina gave the gossiper a coquettish smile. "By saying no."

If she was going to play the role at this gala ushering in the famed Wine Festival, then she might as well go for an Academy Award. She placed her hands beneath her breasts as if adjusting her bra, squirmed in her too tight leather mini, trailed her fingers over her hip and downward, and adjusted the top of her thigh-high boot.

The woman and her cronies gawked, the men ogled, Nina winked and reached for a flute of champagne from the waiter passing by. Cade stood several yards from her deep in conversation with his uncle and, she was sure, not missing a thing.

Soon after they'd arrived, he made the quick intros and left her to the devices of the gossip squad. Every female eye had tracked him crossing the room, before turning a critical eye on her. His potent sexuality and devil-may-care attitude didn't go unnoticed by the female set.

And the scowl he now tossed her way didn't detract from it.

He'd glowered at her ever since he walked back to the shack from the barn, dressed in evening attire. Compared to him, she looked like a high-class call girl strutting the hotel foyer—exactly what she aimed for.

He'd nearly gone ballistic.

"No…oh no." He'd given her the once over, swept up several outfits strewn on the bed by the hearth and tossed them to her. "Get into something else or—"

"Sure, Cade," she murmured, an impish edge to her words. "Will this do?" She held up a skimpier outfit than the one she wore, then scooped up another, dangling it in front of him. "How about this one?"

His dark look seemed to settle in the grooves of his face. "Find something more decent or I'll find it for you." His words crackled, his eyes zeroing on the plunging neckline outlining her bosom. He squinted at the gold chain circling her throat, most of it hidden beneath the back of her dress. "Your necklace seems to have snagged—"

"No." She tottered back a step on her stiletto-heeled boots and slammed her hand at the risqué neckline. The last thing she needed was for him to discover she kept her wedding ring, even if only on a chain around her neck.

He took a menacing step closer. "I'll help—" A snap of his fingers. "Ring." His hawkish gaze glued on her left hand. "Where—"

The sound of the chopper landing smothered his words. Disgruntled at the intrusion, he pivoted, and the momentum fluttered his hair, revealing the gold loop at his earlobe. The proud tilt of his head was so uniquely his and so masculine it had her heart thudding.

The man was too darn attractive, oozing a sexual magnetism that could snare her emotionally and physically if she wasn't on guard.

"I-I have something that might do." She sucked in a breath, and the wardrobe samples slipped from her fingers, pooling on the floor.

"Gotta go." He cast her a censuring look, grabbed her wrist and dragged her with him out to the chopper. "Behave yourself."

Raucous laughter pierced her thoughts, and Nina blinked at the woman who'd flung her the burning question. Sensing monster-size envy from her and her circle, she followed their line of vision back to…Cade.

Cade dressed in black trousers and matching evening jacket with his half-open white shirt offsetting the humid night, stood head and shoulders above the other men. A modern swashbuckling pirate, and she could imagine the fantasies zipping through the female faction, because she had her own x-rated fantasies about the man she married. A sigh struggled from deep within her. And that's what they had to remain. Fantasies.

At that moment, the *Bouzouki* band in the main salon struck up another melody, and the crowd applauded the folk dancers. "*Opa! Bravo!*"

Nina smiled. The party was in full swing. Waiters scurried in and out of the open glass doors, the aroma of lamb roasting on the outdoor rotisseries filled the air and made her mouth water. In the hotel foyer, a champagne waterfall cascaded over ice crystals, misting orchids floating upon the golden pool and charging the ambiance to full throttle.

A couple whirled their way onto the terrace to dance beneath the star-studded sky, spotlighted by the crescent moon hanging low on the horizon. In the distance, Limassol Harbor glittered and a sea breeze sailed in like a lover's caress.

Nina gulped down a sigh. It'd be so easy to cast her cares to the wind and fall in with the romantic fervor. So easy to yield to him. But if she did, she'd be lost; her heart, her career and her chances of extricating her father from those who ruined him.

The champagne bubbles fizzed, and she stared deep into her glass, her shoulders drooping at the monumental task ahead. But she had no recourse. She'd come too close to turn back now. She'd have to return to the village *kafeneon*; but how to do it with Cade and his honchos watching her every move?

She lowered her lashes, keeping Cade point-blank center of

her narrowed focus. He bent his head to listen to his uncle's query, and then tightened his fingers around the glass of *Ouzo*, the traditional anise flavored liqueur. Deep lines etched his face. He tossed the drink back in one gulp, and slammed the glass on a sideboard beneath a mirror on the wall. He turned and clashed with her gaze, his eyes glittering with fury.

She flicked a strand of hair off her shoulder, the motion making her earrings jangle, and purposely batted her eyelashes.

Of course that infuriated him more.

Oblivious to the undertow between Cade and herself, the women at the party munched on *bourekia*—fried dough canapés stuffed with cheese or meat, and swallowed wine like it was water. They jostled her along, their laughter a shrill sound across the crowded room.

Toying with the stem of her glass, Nina glanced about for an escape route and stepped toward the patio. At the same moment, someone touched her arm, and she twisted around. Fear darted through her, but at his reassuring nod, she flashed him a smile and fell into his arms.

Cade frowned, and barely caught the last of his uncle's words.

"…caught the culprit?"

"Closing in."

"Perhaps I can help?"

"I don't need your kind of help." Cade shot him a lethal look and refastened his sights on Nina. But in that split second shift, he'd glimpsed both regret and censure in his uncle's eyes that hurled him back ten years to their explosive confrontation in the Sloan and Sloan boardroom. Cade flexed his shoulder blades, and refused to dwell in the past, preferring to stand grounded in the present.

"Hardheaded as ever," his uncle muttered, then grinned, following his line of vision.

Cade ignored the bait, and watched the stranger waltz Nina out to the terrace. A battering ram struck center of his solar plexus, and he tautened every muscle in his body to offset the unwelcome reaction. Nina, his wife, his—he nearly gagged, but managed to siphon a gallon of oxygen into his lungs—dancing away with this man—his suspect.

"My, these Greeks do enjoy life…*kefi*, they call it." His uncle tossed back his drink, placed the tumbler on a passing waiter's tray and reached for another.

"Yeah." Cade straightened the cuffs of his jacket sleeves and made to stride past him. "If you'll excuse me, *uncle*."

A feather-light touch on his forearm halted him.

"Come, introduce me to your lovely bride." A woman in her fifties looped her arm with his uncle's, her words almost a query.

Cade barely glanced at her, but he caught the wobble in her voice.

A memory nicked his thoughts. He was unable to grasp it, and it dissolved, leaving in its wake a gaping hole. Instinctively, he knew some day he'd have to find out what caused it, but it wouldn't be today.

"Some other time," he said, his words gruff. A shard of ice poked his chest. Shaking his head at the unexpected jab, he strode onto the terrace and at the sight of Nina, the ice melted.

She was alone.

Relief blasted through him, then a myriad of other feelings. Not wanting to plow through the reason his heart thudded like a sledgehammer on steel girders, he pushed them aside. She was leaning against the banister, staring out to sea, and he wanted to wrap his arms around her, toss her over his shoulder and march to his lair, to keep her close, feeling her against him, to—

Caveman tactics would not work here, Cade.

A raw sound burst from him, and he stepped nearer.

She spun around and choking the champagne flute between her fingers, made to sidestep him.

"Running away already?" he challenged.

She laughed, a brittle sound. "Hardly, with your hounds on the prowl."

He didn't pretend not to understand what she referred to. "Just ensuring my asset stays intact…er…stays put." He tempered his words with a grin, but his unyielding tone didn't go amiss.

"I did not break the deal." Once more, she made to push past him but he stepped up at the same moment so her breasts bumped his chest.

She drew in a sharp breath.

He expelled his in force.

"You did," she accused.

He lifted a brow in query.

"Don't play the innocent," Nina fired, attacking the enemy. "I heard you on the phone the day of our wedding."

He shook his head. "That was over a year ago."

"Let me refresh your memory." Her mouth felt dry and her pulse raced. But she didn't care. She was out to let rip what she'd been holding in for far too long. She licked her lips.

His brows knitted, and a cyclone brewed in his eyes.

Danger crackled in the air.

"Then it's true," he baited, his hips touching hers.

"What?" The word a breath of sound, the ocean breeze a balm to her tattered nerves.

She'd sensed him the moment he stepped up behind her; the subtle scent of his cologne a trigger to her emotions. Prickles erupted on her spine and spread all over her body. Her stomach did funny things, her lungs ached for oxygen and her palms dampened. A droplet slid between her breasts, seeping into her bra. She wanted to both lean back into his powerful frame and run from him.

"That women don't forget a thing."

"You're the expert."

He cocked his head to the side.

"Your mug was plastered on the front page of practically every New York magazine with your latest conquest."

"Media's out to sell copy. Scandal sells." He grazed his cheek with the back of his hand. "Don't believe everything you read."

"I don't."

A smile split his mouth, and he placed his finger under her chin, lifting it up so she had to look at him. "But it bothered you?"

"Couldn't care less." She swatted his hand away.

"And so that's why you married me?" he asked, his body still touching hers, his heat shooting into her and heightening her senses.

"I married you because—" She broke off realizing he almost got a confession out of her she wasn't ready to give.

"You married me because of the million plus that filled your greedy little palm." He gripped her shoulders, his breath ruffling wisps of hair at her temple. "And that was the tip of the iceberg, compared to what you'd pull in, working from the inside, married to me."

She jerked in his arms.

"Hit a nerve, have I?" he bit out, his query icing her flesh even in the balmy Mediterranean night. "You'll pay off what you stole and deliver the crackman...your accomplice."

"I don't know what you're talking about," she snapped, but her voice dipped.

"The guy in the village—"

"No!"

"—wouldn't be your dancing partner?" he said, his eyes like Arctic ice.

She gasped for air.

He blasted out a breath.

"He means that much to you?"

"Yes...no." She twisted the ring on her finger; she'd managed to slip it on when she dashed back to the shack for her purse seconds before take-off. "Please don't, Cade."

"Please don't what, Cade?" he bit back, his words fierce, noting her motion.

"It's not your business."

He laughed, a dry sound. "What belongs to me is sure as heck my business, sweetheart." He trailed his fingers through her hair, and cupped her cheek, grazing the sensitive pulse point at her throat.

"He has nothing that is yours, Cade."

He outlined her mouth with his fingertip, the pad of his thumb brushing her bottom lip. "I'll make sure of it."

"What's that supposed to mean?" His touch did things to her insides, her nerves; her heart lunged, then sped. She gulped some champagne, it went down the wrong way, and she sputtered.

"You okay?" He patted her back.

"Yes," she wheezed, and staggered back a step, the balcony rail pressing into her back.

"Sure?"

She nodded, and plunked the glass on a nearby table. She blinked at the moonlight shimmering on his face, accentuating the planes and shadows of his features...a warrior's face; strong, powerful—merciless.

Cade drew closer, pressing his advantage so tightly his thighs skimmed the material of her dress.

She started, and something indefinable skittered across his gaze.

"Now how did I break the deal?" He lowered his mouth, his voice husky, his breath teasing her lips.

"You never intended to go through with it." She swallowed, her words sounding sluggish even to her own ears.

"You mean this?" He shifted and his mouth crushed hers.

She pressed her hands against his torso—a barricade, but his body heat permeated his shirt, singeing her fingertips. The feel of silk beneath her palms spiked the sensual assault on her mouth; gliding her hands up and across his chest, she looped her arms around his neck.

His kiss rocked her to her toes, and she held on to him, the hair at his nape tickling her knuckles. And then, he deepened the intimate connection ... his tongue slid into her mouth, stroked... invited...and she accepted, swaying with him to the waltz of the senses.

Just for a moment, she lost herself in their passion...in him. Then a cargo ship out in the harbor blew its horn, the sound piercing. She swung her hand out to shove him back and instead knocked the champagne glass off the table. It crashed to the floor and alcohol fumes filled the air.

"L-let go, please." She sucked oxygen into her lungs, the wine-spiked air stinging her throat.

Silence. Dark. Foreboding.

He inclined his head, his breathing labored. "If that's what you want." He held onto her for a moment longer, then let her go, the force of his denial making her totter back against the banister.

The sea crashed upon the rocks, a crescendo of nature's fury. A lover's melody drifted out to them. Everything seemed to conspire against her resisting him. Her pulse leaped into her throat, and she gasped for air.

He skewered her with his granite gaze.

A tremor zipped through her, and she wrapped her arms about herself. "I don't intend to be another notch on your stud belt—"

"Enough." He set his jaw.

But she wasn't done, not by a long shot. She wanted to strike out at him because she hurt…hurt being so near him, yet hurt at the distance between them that was like a chasm.

"—married to you or not."

"Now there's an interesting statement."

She curled her fingers around the rail behind her, the metal imprinting her flesh.

"Being hitched brings with it some—" –a glint in his eye, a killer smile on his mouth— "conjugal rights."

She drew in a sharp breath that scalded her throat.

"And I intend to collect mine. Tonight."

"Oh really?"

"Mmm, unless you wanna amend the agreement?"

"What d' you mean?"

"Tag the hacker and I'll cancel the note you owe me," he said, his laser-sharp focus drilling into her. "Or pay up in more creative ways."

You schmuck…you think you'll get into her confidence with those tactics?

"Go to—"

"I wouldn't keep referring to that—not a nice place." His gut recoiled at memories bombarding his brain, every muscle in his body taut.

She pushed past him, and that snapped him from his thoughts.

"I take it that's a no on both counts?" he said, attempting a lighter tone.

But when she kept walking, he bridged the gap in two strides and grabbed her arm. "Where do you think you're going at this time of night?"

"Away from this toxic atmosphere." She jerked her arm from his grasp. "I need some fresh air." She meandered around him and breezed down the stairs.

Well okay, maybe he had that coming, but his male ego rebelled against her walking out on him again.

Her perfume lingered in the air. A nerve slugged his jaw and worked its way down his neck to his shoulder blades. He watched her cross the gardens to the parking lot. In her haste, she stumbled, caught her balance and checked her boot. She limped through the massive wrought-iron gate, disappearing around the hedge of bougainvillea.

Cade shot into action, signaling his chauffeur with a wave of his hand.

******

Nina limped along the citrus-tree lined boulevard, and the eerie sound of the sea lapping the shore had her glancing over her shoulder. Except for the moonbeam lighting her path, she was surrounded by darkness. Foolish to have been so impulsive and—

Someone bumped into her, and she stifled a scream.

The shoeless couple giggled, slipping and sliding their way down the slope to the beach, the smell of booze and the sound of belching tainting the atmosphere.

Nina picked up her pace, and then stopped her awkward gait. What was she doing? Where was she going? There were no cabs or buses this far out of town, and she had no idea how many miles she'd have to traipse to get to public transport.

An owl hooted, and she froze. A flutter of wings and the bird flew off. She chuckled at her idiotic imaginings. An unsteady breath and she trekked on. She didn't go two steps when headlights from behind caught her in the beam of light. Spinning around, she raised a hand to shield her eyes and hugged the shoulder of the road until the car passed.

But the vehicle swerved to a stop several feet ahead of her and blocked her path. Danger signals shimmied up her spine, her pulse racing, her breath shallow, rasping. She glanced about.

Behind her, the estate was ablaze with lights, the sounds of music barely audible this far out. She couldn't sprint for it. With her tight miniskirt and missing stiletto heel, she'd fall flat on her face. In front of her, the moonlight turned the deserted road into Spook Street. She bit her lip, caught between indecision, but when the car door opened, she poised for flight.

"Get in." Cade's clipped command stopped her in motion.

But just for a second.

"No." She backed away, and her foot slid down the embankment. Loose soil and pebbles sounded like an avalanche in the stillness of the night bar the purr of the engine.

Cade lunged, seizing her elbow. "Another foot or two and I'd have to fish you from the bay." He motioned toward the hush of surf. "Ditto my chauffeur dragging the intoxicated couple from plunging—"He shook his head. A lock of hair flopped on his forehead, and he bashed it back with his hand. "Not two feet from you is a ledge with a sheer drop to the ocean. The warning sign is invisible in the dark."

Reaction rattled her, and she mouthed back, "I'll take my chances—"

"Don't be foolish." He hooked his arm around her waist and slung her over his shoulder.

She kicked her feet in the air and swung her arms at him, but missed. And that had her boiling mad. "Put me down, you—you—"

"Sure thing." He plunked her down in the front seat of the limo and slid into the driver's seat. "Buckle up, babe." A moment, and he pressed on the gas pedal, zooming off.

"Where're we going?"

"Home." He tossed her a glance, and she averted her face, glaring out at the night whizzing by.

Nina blinked the blur of tears from her eyes. Home. If that were only true. But it was distant as that star in the sky, twinkling on its lonesome.

"What, no 'thank you' for saving your life?" he asked, tongue-in-cheek.

She favored him with what sounded like a snort.

He chuckled. "Okay, so you can say thank you later."

She flounced further from him in the confining space.

"In bed."

CHAPTER SEVEN

It was past midnight when Cade carried her over the threshold of their village abode, booting the door shut behind him. Slung over his shoulder, Nina felt like a sack of potatoes, and itching to strike out at him, thought it smarter to play possum.

Without pausing to turn on the light, he flung her on the bed, his breath a rush of sound in the quiet of night. She kept her eyes closed, hoping he'd march out to the barn, and then, she'd leap up and make her escape.

Ding, ding! The dong sounded the replay of a year ago in her brain. Somehow she didn't think it'd be so easy this time around.

"Sleeping beauty," he murmured, his words a warm caress upon her skin. When she remained motionless, except for the rise and fall of her breasts, he gathered her in his embrace. Her face was pressed against his shirt, his heart thrashing in her ear, his male scent an aphrodisiac. He shifted, and his half-open shirt gaped open, her mouth brushing his chest.

Erotic. And dangerous.

He steeled his arms about her, and then relaxed, one hand stroking her nape, the other fumbling for the zipper of her dress.

She held her breath.

He unzipped her dress.

Her heart rate hiked off the map.

He paused at the base of her spine.

A reprieve. But was it? She wanted him to continue.

He glided his hands along the curve of her hip to her thigh and pulled off her boot, his fingers trailing down her leg to her ankle until her foot nestled in his palm.

Heat suffused her body, her lungs about to explode.

A sigh of relief when he massaged the arch of her foot, sensitizing her nerves to a fervor of tingles. He removed her other boot and pulled an object from his jacket pocket.

"This yours?" he asked, his voice gravelly.

"Mmm." She nodded, barely opening her lashes. The stiletto heel she'd broken in her dash through the car park, held in his palm.

He set it on the floor beside her boot, and placed his hands on her shoulders, his thumbs stroking the pulse points at her neck. Slow as molasses, he shimmied the dress off her shoulders and down to her waist.

Cold air brushed her skin, a direct contrast to the heat of his touch, and goose bumps erupted on her body.

Cade drew in a sharp breath, and his hands shook. Her breasts were adorned in lace, their nipples straining for his touch. Moonlight shimmered through the half open shutters, casting light and shadow on her. Over this delectable female who was his…not technically, but legally. Caution flashed through his mind, but it was overridden by erotic fantasies about this woman he held in his hands, had in his care, in his keeping.

Ignoring the reservations bombarding his brain, he could still enjoy her; after all, she'd not only quipped 'I do' but cashed out on him. Every sinew in his body tightened, his lungs constricted, and he blasted out a breath.

Payback.

And this is how you want it? He locked his mind against the attack of his conscience. *With her?* The thought persisted. *A quickie on the fly?*

Shut up.

An act of seduction?

He clamped down on the irritants, tuning in to his body's reaction, his heart— a muscle clubbed his chest.

Bunching her dress in his hands, he pushed it lower, his fingers tensing over the material, his blood heating. The trinket at her navel gleamed, and he was hard pressed not to dip his head, fusing his mouth to the spot and flirting with his tongue.

He nudged the fabric over her hips and down her thighs, and he almost buckled at the knees. A silk scrap of nothing covered the shadow between her thighs, fueling his libido. He gulped down his lust, for of course that's all it could be, he reminded himself, blocking the niggle in his brain. With a swift flick of his fingers, he discarded the dress from her body.

Air filled his lungs, and he closed his eyes, allowing it to sizzle from his lips.

He pulled the covers back, stole another glance at the goddess in his bed and draped the blanket over her. He brushed his thumb along the curve of her cheek to her mouth, outlining her lips… soft, moist…he could almost taste—

She opened her mouth and nipped his thumb.

"Hey." He snatched his hand away and caught the glint of mischief in her eyes.

Or was that a dare?

"Move over, wife."

Nina was wound up like a spring ready to come unhinged; her pulse skyrocketed. His touch lingered on her mouth, and she licked her lips, tasting him. But doubts zoomed in her brain. To him she was just another woman, regardless if she was married to him or not. Was this a way for him to salve his ego?

And could she allow it? Something inside her stirred, but she paid it no heed. Maybe just this once, she could forget their differences and partake in the forbidden pleasure he offered.

The hush of sound as he removed his shirt reached her, and she peeked at him from beneath her lashes. Her body blushed with anticipation, then cooled with fear. Not of him, but what her reaction would reveal to him; what she suspected, but didn't want to admit even to herself. She burrowed beneath the covers and hugged the pillow, smothering a moan.

Was she falling for this guy? That was something that she couldn't allow.

He unbuckled his belt and sat on the edge of the bed, the mattress depressing beneath his weight.

She held her breath, her heart thudding, knowing, *you couldn't love to order.*

And afterward? Her mind shot back. *Who's going to pick up the pieces?*

Before she could formulate an answer, he reclined and reached for her. Her stomach clenched, she swallowed, and a kick of emotion zinged through her. She was about to open her arms to him, when his cell phone beeped, puncturing the silence of the room. She muffled a nervous giggle.

A heavy beat.

It beeped again.

An expletive incinerated the air.

He grabbed his jacket from the floor, yanked the phone from the pocket and flipped it open. "Sloan."

A moment ticked by, and he shot her a covert glance. "You've located him?"

Nina's eyes flew open, and she drew the blanket up to her chin, the chill invading her body and freezing her bones. Caught whom? Her father?

"Sure it's him?"

A grim stillness.

He met and held her gaze, hesitated, then, "On my way."

A regrettable sigh, and he stroked her cheek with his fingers. "You can relax," he murmured, but an underlying seriousness belied his mocking tone. "You'll be sleeping alone tonight."

A moonbeam cast light and shadow on his body…strong, virile, powerful.

Sexual.

He was all male, a rare man, this man she married. Nina heard the swish of clothes as he got dressed. She slammed her eyes shut, gulping down disappointment, but it was quickly doused by his harsh words.

"Get coffee brewing…this won't take long." His words clipped, his tone cool. "You've got one reprieve"-he paused, allowing his eyes to skim over her—"but you'll make up for it when I get back." He swept his jacket off the bed, his body rigid, his mouth tight. "And you can quit the sleeping beauty routine."

Tension vibrated between them, the connection charged with high wattage emotion.

"You will deliver, *yeneka mou*, wife." He bit the word out like it was poison on his tongue. "And you will initiate it."

She flinched and drew the covers over her head.

His chuckle compounded her ire, her impassioned words of denial muffled beneath the bedding.

"With the brew, my breakfast, *agape mou*." He strode to the door, the sound of his footsteps echoing back to her. "Make sure the eggs are fresh from the chicken coop, the bacon sliced from the slab in the fridge and the toast from oven-baked bread." A pause at the door and, "Freshly squeezed orange juice right from the tree."

He unlatched the door. "Oh, and don't forget to make some for yourself."

At his parting shot, Nina could no longer curb her tongue. She flung the blanket off her face, bolted upright and clutched the bedcovers over her bosom. "Concern for me?" A brittle laugh, then a break in her voice.

"I don't want you fainting"-he tossed her a dark look, and his words shot straight into her heart—"doing my laundry, ironing my shirts, shining my boots—"

"You horrible man." She punched the pillow with her fist and the motion made the blanket slide, exposing her breasts. Instantly, she jerked it back, a flush suffusing her features, and bit her lip.

A hiss of sound from his side of the room, then, "—and warming my bed."

"Oh, you—" She squeezed the pillow in her hands and took aim.

He laughed, but the sound held no amusement. "Think you can handle that?"

She hurled the pillow at him, but by then he'd slipped out the door, and it landed on the wooden planks, plopping to the floor.

A deafening silence followed his exit, then his chuckle filtered back to her, stoking her indignation and prompting her to action.

Muttering a string of unsavory adjectives, Nina pounded her hands and feet upon the mattress, venting her anger.

Five seconds flat.

The rhythm of her breathing vibrated around her. She flicked her hair from her eyes, tossed the blankets aside and leaped from the bed. In her agitation, she didn't even feel the cool air smacking her nude body, and marched to the makeshift closet, rifling through her suitcase. She threw on a pair of jeans, a loose fitting blouse and slipped her feet into sandals.

She stepped to the kitchen shelf, grabbed a rubber band from the dish, and fastened her hair in a ponytail. A glance at her clothes strewn on the floor and the mussed bed, and her pulse skittered. She debated, and then turned away—she'd tidy up later.

She had to get to him before Cade and his thugs.

Snatching her purse off the floor, then her hat, she stole out of the door and clicked it shut behind her. Dawn was just breaking, and scents of jasmine laced the air. A deep breath, a burst of sound from her mouth, and she took off at a run.

"Track her." Grim-faced, Cade stepped from the shadows, signaled his security and sprinted for the chopper. "I want a report on her every move, action, step."

✶✶✶✶✶

Nina pounded on the *kafeneon's* door, her heart lodging in her throat every time she heard a sound. Sleepy-eyed, her father cracked the door open and a woman's voice filtered through. "Who is it?"

Nina gaped. "You're kidding?"

"Got in a couple of hours ago." Sheepishly, her father grinned and offered a quick explanation. He started to say something further, stopped and motioned her inside.

Nina shook her head. Not wanting to intrude on their reunion, she rose on tiptoe and kissed his cheek. "Say hi to mom." On high alert, she backed away. "I'll see you guys later."

But would she? she thought, dashing into the shadows after he closed the door.

She squatted on a brick wall, beneath a gnarled olive tree and kept sentry. A grin curved her mouth. After all these years, her mother finally knew it wasn't another woman, but circumstances that had torn them apart. Determined to stand by her man, she came to Cyprus with the money he'd given Nina to send her. She could no longer allow him to go through the persecution alone.

Birds chirped at the dawning of a new day.

Nina rubbed her arms to ward off the early morning chill, as joy zipped through her.

She yawned, and her eyelids drooped. Fighting to stay awake, she pinched her cheeks and bounced off the wall, the gravel crunching beneath her sandals. A pebble slid inside her shoe. She shook her foot, dislodged the irritant, and wished she could do the same with the man she'd gotten embroiled with.

She sighed and paced, maintaining her vigil. After a couple of hours dragged by, and no one had come for her father, Nina circled back through the market on her way to the hovel she shared with Cade.

She knew a face-off with him was imminent.

65

CHAPTER EIGHT

"You lost her?" Cade was ready to burst a blood vessel, what with high tech tracking devices at their disposal. "Aerial surveillance spies she's still in the vicinity."

A text message dinged his cell phone.

"Find her," he snarled into the transmitter, signaling the pilot to circle back. "I want a full report."

He skimmed the text message and frowned. Why was his uncle texting: **You're off course, target closer to home?** He keyed in his uncle's Limassol office to ace the memo—he'd flown to London. A blast of frustration sounded from deep in his chest. Something was going down, and he had to find out what it was.

The chopper landed, and Cade vaulted out, rolling his shoulders to ease the tension. He inhaled, filling his lungs with pine- scented air. A whiff of citrus blossom…and cooking.

His stomach rumbled. He jogged to the shack, burst through the door and skidded to a halt.

"Hello darling." Nina waved a spatula at him and cracked two eggs in the pan sizzling with olive oil. "Over easy?" She flipped them and smacked them with the spatula, imagining it to be his back.

"Yeah, over easy works." He marched across the room, threw a file on the table and set his laptop beside it.

Nina sensed his foul mood, and turning to more pleasant thoughts, suppressed a giggle tickling her throat.

Who'd have imagined her parents reconnecting after all these years? Then she sobered. Someone *had* set her father up.

She glanced at Cade flicking through the file on the table, and blew a wayward wisp off her brow.

Mere hours ago, her father hinted his long time associate was about to expose the perpetrator; but before he could tell her more, a car motor revved, and she'd sprinted for the shadows.

Nina placed two bread slices in the toaster and opened the icebox.

He'd 'abandoned' them to protect them from the backlash, and weathered the blackmail alone; still sheltering them from the onslaught massing on the horizon.

She forked bacon slices from the package, shouldered the icebox shut and dropped them in the pan. Oil sputtered, and she took a step back. She scooped the eggs onto a plate and gave her husband a veiled glance.

Could Cade be behind her father's persecution? An ache throbbed inside her, and she gripped the counter, bracing against the possibility. Air left her lungs. She flipped the bacon, and her lip quivered.

After she'd left the *kafeneon* near dawn, she slipped by Cade's men milling near the marketplace, and hurried 'home'…thinking of him.

Her father.

A wanted man.

Who she could set free and right the past, but if she could only get Cade to listen. Listen to her. She had to find a way. Even if it meant—

Her pulse skittered, and her chest tightened. Could she risk her heart?

Wouldn't that be replacing one casualty for another—her? She crunched down the jitters. She had to do it. Her father's freedom and her mother's happiness depended on her taking that risk.

"Bacon crisp?"

She fought back the sting of tears. They'd already lost twelve years all because of—

"Crisp will do," Cade muttered, without so much as a glance her way.

She blinked, refocused on the task at hand and forced a smile on her face. "How was your day, dear?"

His scowl darkened. "Maybe I should ask you the same thing, mmm?"

"Ask away." She shrugged, her tone flippant, thus aggravating him more. Served him right, after what he'd put her through. And she wasn't done yet. "But I already know what that's about."

Suspicion tinted his eyes. "You do?"

"You're disappointed." She transferred the bacon onto the plate of eggs, placed the pan in the sink and set the kettle on to boil. "The eggs are from the fridge not the coop, the bacon from the market not the butcher's slab and the juice from the can not the orange tree."

"Where've you been?" He bridged the gap in two strides and stood behind her, his breath ruffling the curls at her nape.

Prickles rose on her skin, her hands went moist, and she wanted to lean back into him, his muscled chest, to rest, to—

The toast popped up. She snatched the slices from the toaster and slapped them on the plate. "And the bread's from the bakery not—"

"And why's that?"

"No time to bake this morning."

"Because?"

She swung past him, placed the plate on the table, rerouted for the demitasse, swerved by him and set it on the table with the orange juice. "I went shopping."

"For?"

"Whatever do you mean?" She sucked in a breath, her heart thudding. He stepped up, wedging her against the table, his thighs brushing her buttocks and sending shimmers of sensation through her. Her hand glided across the table, and a spoon clattered to the floor. She started.

"Nervous?"

"No-o." She wiggled for breathing room, but it only caused friction between them.

"Honey, you keep doing that, and we'll land right here on the floor—"

She bent down for the spoon, and her tush smacked into his groin.

He sucked in a blizzard of air.

A sweet jab of sensation pierced her to the core.

She seized the utensil and bolted upright so fast, her head cracked his chin.

"Ouch," he grumbled, and she skipped away from him.

He paced her every move.

She dropped the spoon in the sink, swallowed and swiped her palms on the front of her jeans.

"Ketchup?" She reached for a bottle from the cupboard and her shirt rode up.

He stepped up.

"Very nice." He slid his hands around her bare midriff, nuzzling her neck, sparking fine hair at her nape.

"I-I thought it'd add zing to your breakfast."

He chuckled, his breath a fizz of fever on her skin. Sizzle shot into her, and her head lolled back onto his shoulder. Just for a heartbeat, she stayed there; his heat, his touch stirred her senses, and a sigh feathered from her mouth. Just for a second, she imagined...but abruptly she twisted to push him away and fell into his gaze.

Cade lowered his head, and his lips melded with hers...tender, moist, sweet sensation charged into her. She curved into his embrace. He tightened his arms around her, jamming her hard against him, his erection pressing into her. Her stomach dipped.

She sucked in a breath from his mouth, her nipples skimming his chest. He slid his tongue into her mouth, withdrew slightly, then penetrated further… the motion reflecting the rhythm of his hips against hers.

Lost in the sensual promise of that kiss, Nina moaned; her heart beating a frenzied tempo to the erotic waltz in her mouth. A guttural sound vibrated from deep in his throat. He bunched her hair in his hands, held her head steady and ravished her mouth.

The shrill whistle of the kettle—a douche of ice water—and she stilled in his arms. "Y-your breakfast's getting cold."

"And we're anything but, baby doll," he murmured, his words a breath of sound against her lips. Curving an arm around her, he turned off the stove. "We're about to combust in a blaze, right here, right now."

He cupped her breast with one hand and her buttocks with the other, pulling her hard against his aroused strength. A flick of his thumb across her nipple, and a whimper of pleasure echoed deep in her throat. He dipped his head, suckling the orb in his mouth, fabric and all.

She gasped, and her head flopped onto his shoulder. On the brink of surrender, a shudder frisked through her and—

The Greek coffee boiled over and splattered on the stove.

"Your coffee's ready." She pushed against him, but her hands felt limp and powerless.

"And so are we." He lifted his head, his mouth a feather breadth from hers, his ragged breath singeing her lips. "Primed and ready."

The inferno ignited into a blaze.

She leaned into him, unable to stop, wanting him to—

A knock on the door.

A rooster crowed.

She turned in his arms, her head resting on his shoulder, and siphoned a mouthful of air. He tightened his arms about her, his breath like a typhoon in her ear. A million jabs of sensation zapped into her, and she almost cried. She bashed down the whimper ebbing in her throat and tore away from his embrace, the emotional aftershocks pulsing through her.

"You better wash up…coffee…your breakfast," she broke off realizing she was rambling. "My tea."

The banging on the door grew louder.

Cade uttered a blue streak beneath his breath, stalked to the door and nearly wrenched it off its hinges.

Like an automaton, Nina staggered to the stove, turned off the burner and gripped the coffee pot. A whiff of the strong brew—a wake-up call. She managed to walk back to the table on boneless legs and poured the coffee in his cup, spilling only a drop or two.

A murmured exchange from the doorway, with 'report' being the only decipherable word drifting to her.

An ominous silence.

Cade shut the door and turned, his features chiseled granite, his eyes stone cold.

A tremor ripped through her. What did he know?

Cade bridged the distance between them in two strides and slapped a folder on the table. Taciturn, he marched to the sink, poured water from the jug into his palm, his grip on the ceramic handle iron-hard.

Why hadn't she told him? He batted hair off his brow with an impatient hand, water spraying the air. The caveman tactics hadn't worked. Instead of opening up to him, she had clammed up.

Only her body spoke to him. It was in rhythm with his, conducting symphony of their senses.

It was proof that she wasn't averse to his touch. The sensual interlude they shared moments ago had his blood pulsing hot through his veins and sent his heart rate into high gear. He snatched a towel from the rack, dried his hands, hurled it on the countertop and strode back to her.

She stood immobilized, her eyes wide…vulnerable pools of emotion, uncertain yet alert. She glanced at the door over his shoulder, seeming to gauge the distance.

"Uh, uh." He tapped the folder, inclined his head for her to sit down, and wondered why he didn't let her run out with a 'hasta la vista, babe' as had been his original intent. A shifting inside him, and a stab in his heart gave him pause, but he savagely resisted the pull of the sentiment.

"Better hurry and grab a bite," he said, his words harsh, almost cruel. "We've a long trip ahead of us."

Her head snapped up. "We're leaving?"

He hooked a chair with his boot, scraped it back and straddled it.

"London." The hacker had created a maze from New York to Cyprus to London. How Florence, Italy fitted into his scheme Cade wasn't sure yet, but he'd find out. He had to…because of her.

He sent a covert glance her way. Had he connected all the dots? The hacker was about to cyber-launder the funds via key global financial institutions to cover his tracks. Unless they compromised his plan in a sting operation, he'd jet off to parts unknown again.

"You go." She pushed her hands in the back pockets of her jeans and the fabric of her shirt stretched taut across her breasts.

He eclipsed the growl deep in his chest with his fist.

"I don't have to go." She tossed her head in defiance.

"Oh, but you do."

"Why?"

"Overdue honeymoon." His eyes held hers for an endless beat, and then his mouth tilted in a provocative grin. He picked up a piece of toast and bit into it with gusto. "Eat up, it's a long trip."

"I've lost my appetite." She marched past him, but he shot an arm out, grabbing her wrist and pulling her onto his lap.

"Well, I haven't." A wicked lift to his brow.

"For what?" She leaped to her feet, putting distance between them.

"Your services." He tore off another piece of toast with his teeth, took a gulp of coffee and held the cup out to her.

She grabbed the pot from the table and poured the last of the brew in his cup. "Will that be all, your royal jerkins?"

"No." He pierced a piece of egg, placed it in his mouth, chewed and swallowed. "I've been up all night"—he swished a finger around his shirt collar— "run my bath will you, honey."

She shook her head, befuddled. "There's no bathtub here, the outside shower—"

"Quite right." He punctured a slab of bacon, popped it in his mouth and chomped, swallowed. "You can wash my back then."

"Huh!" She stamped to the stove, slammed the lid on the pan in the sink, tossed in the cutlery and closed her fingers over the towel he'd left on the counter.

"A massage prior to—" He rolled his shoulders and palmed his nape. "Hey!" He ducked in the nick of time, the missile whizzing over his head and smacking the wall.

A glint in his eye, then he shrugged, which stoked her ire.

"Perhaps you're right." He stuffed another forkful of food in his mouth, chomped and gulped down the coffee. "No time." He blotted his mouth with the napkin. "You'll administer the magic of your touch when we get to London."

CHAPTER NINE

"Take a memo Ms...er...Mrs. Sloan." Cade lounged on the plush sofa of their penthouse at the Park Lane Hotel in Mayfair, nursing a drink in his hands.

"What?" Nina swung around from viewing London lights reflected on the Thames River in the distance. Big Ben struck the ninth hour, and soon it'd be bedtime ...she swayed...with her espoused enemy. She rubbed goose bumps from her arms, not sure whether the reaction was caused by alarm or anticipation.

"After tonight, you'll make strides in reducing the principal and interest on the note."

She sucked in a sharp breath, scoring her throat, and for a moment remained speechless, trying to wrap her mind around the implication of his words.

"Be thankful, rates are low." He took a swig of the drink and smacked his lips. "Or annual interest accrued be astronomical."

"You're despicable."

"Go change," he snarled. "Dinner *a deux* on the terrace."

"I'm not hungry." She didn't move.

He raised the glass to his mouth, glanced at the dining table over the rim, then at her, his meaning unmistakable. "Room service then?" Setting the tumbler down on the sidebar, he hauled himself from the sofa, and rapped his knuckles on the glossy tabletop. "Sturdy."

She slid her hands in the back pockets of her jeans and took a step back, her eyes wide, and her lashes fluttering. Her heart thumping with...

Expectancy.

Excitement.

His brows knitted over the bridge of his nose. He propped his hip on the table's edge and folded his arms across his chest. "The dinner meeting with the VIP" –he paused, gauging her reaction— "and former employee of Sloan Global Corp. had to be rescheduled."

"Meeting...former employee?" She sounded dimwitted even to her own ears, the query a sliver of sound from her mouth.

"Yep."

"No." She retreated a step, hooked her thumbs on her denim waistband and anchored her back against the wall. He could only mean her father, but how'd he known? A raw sound gurgled from her throat, and she smothered it with the back of her hand. Of course. How foolish of her. Cade Sloan didn't miss a thing; not with his henchmen and his high tech tracking devices trailing her to the village.

"We could forego dinner altogether." He waggled his shoulders, his gaze straying over her, and loosened a couple of buttons of his designer shirt.

Hot sizzle shot into her, and she tried to counter the pull of his sexuality with a verbal attack. "You know, don't you?" She brushed moist palms on her tush and looked him straight in the eye. "This cat and mouse game you've been playing was just to...to—"

"Catch you?" His eyes glittered like agates, skewering her. "In secret assignations with a man at the village taverna?"

She paled. "*Kafeneon*," she murmured the inconsequential correction. "You know who he is?"

"Not personally, yet," he ground out, his vague answer unnerving. "Suffice to say, you will not be meeting him again."

"What have you done to him?" A sinister thought hurled through her mind, and she tore at him, her arms flailing. "If you've hurt him—"

He caught her arms, binding her wrists between his fingers, his thumbs stroking her pulse points. The tension between them built to combustible levels. Her breath mingled with his, sounding harsh and heavy in the fleeting hush between them.

"Hurt is relative," he murmured. "Pain can be many things."

She struggled in his grasp, her Jimmy Choos kicking his shins.

"Be still, woman." He wrapped his arms around her and hauled her against his chest, holding her so tightly she couldn't move. Her pulse beat a fast and furious tempo with his. A gasp of oxygen, a flick of her tongue. and she tasted the salty moisture glazing her upper lip.

A rumble sounded deep in his throat, then it blasted in a gush of air from his mouth.

"That's why you wanted to come to London." She slammed her heel on his loafer and shoved him back.

"Ouch," he grumbled. He made to reach for her, changed his mind and let her stew.

That got her more prickly. "Oh!" She threw her hands up in the air and marched a weave around the furniture. And here she thought the flight from Larnaca to London and the limo ride from Heathrow, except for a quick cell call he made, had been uneventful.

All the while he'd been plotting. She stamped full circle and stopped mere inches from him. "This posh suite, the champagne in the ice bucket, the fruit basket, the gowns in the closet, the jewelry...shoes." He knew she had a weakness for designer footwear.

"You like it all." A statement, not a query.

"No." The word exploded between them.

He watched her through his blade-thin focus.

"All this" –she waved her hand about— "was to set the seduction scene. To entice, to lure..."

A slither of sound between his teeth.

"...get me away from him," she accused, her words a whimper. "Pump me for information against my own fa—" she stuttered to a stop when he stalked to the bedroom.

Her head buzzed. But her father hadn't mentioned London during those few minutes she'd seen him at the crack of dawn. What was going on?

Could she have missed—

"Fifteen minutes." Cade strode back out and tossed a Valentino silk dress to her. "*I am* hungry."

Nina hurled the dress back. It bounced off his chest and floated to the floor at his feet. Obviously he had his own agenda, and until she knew his schemata, she'd play for time.

"You can't buy me."

He lifted a brow. "Really?"

She blinked, her mind befuddled for a second. "Th-that was different."

His eyes brewed a storm, the signal clear; he didn't believe her.

Well, maybe she couldn't blame him in the circumstances. She had scooped the loot and skipped town a year ago. But it had been her share, so she wouldn't feel guilty.

"You can't make me say anything...do..." Her voice wobbled, but she angled her head in defiance. "No matter what you do... after all this time, we're finally together. I love him. He's my—"

And that lit the fuse beneath his controlled demeanor. "You dare flaunt another man in my face?" He booted the dress in her direction, and she let it fly past her.

Realizing her mistake in provoking him, she reached out to him with outstretched arms. "It's not what you think—"

"To give him what's mine...what I bought?"

"*What?*" Something wilted inside her, and she dropped her arms to her sides. He considered her to be an item, a possession; at least he could have referred to her as a *who*. "I'm not a *thing* and you didn't buy—"

"Pardon." He had the class to apologize, and she bristled. She wanted to pile the negatives against him, so she could find an excuse to hate him. "Who," he muttered. "I did buy...you. For a million and a half...for one night, remember?"

She stumbled back a step and gripped the edge of the table, the slick hardwood pressing into her fingertips.

He advanced.

She held her breath.

His features hardened.

Her breath fizzed from her mouth.

He placed his hands on her shoulders, his eyes welded to hers, and he drew her to him. His chest chafed her breasts and his thighs grazed hers, his solid strength pressing into her. Sweet sensation arrowed through her, pooling in her female vortex, and she wondered how she could deny the attraction, even to protect her vulnerability.

"I'm not yours." She struck his chest with her fist, but he didn't budge.

She squirmed. All her resistance couldn't camouflage her body's reaction to him. Her flesh flamed. She'd been dormant for so long, and his touch awakened feelings she'd long suppressed. Feelings… for him. But she couldn't give in, not until she knew what was to become of her father.

Suddenly, she realized what she'd done. She'd just admitted to herself she had feelings for Cade. Her awareness of his presence immediately became more acute, and the sexual tension intensified between them. Her body throbbed. She opened her eyes wide, then dipped her lashes, her pulse scrambling.

He shifted in place. A crack in his armor?

It was a chasm. A chasm birthed from the veneer they'd both maintained for over a year. Too long. A life sentence.

"Cade," she whispered, his name a soft caress. Reaching up, she touched his cheek, his bristles scouring her palm.

Stimulating.

She stroked him with her fingertips; to tame the tiger he unleashed everytime she battled him, fueling explosive feelings between them. Feelings she could no longer deny.

"Wha…who I've paid for." He stuttered, but even he was past rational thought.

She lowered her hand to his chest.

Heat.

His heat scalded her fingers, but she endured, keeping that bare inch of space between them.

For her sanity.

If he pursued further, she'd fall into him...his passion...and hers. She'd be lost.

"I-I don't carry a price tag," she murmured, her heart sinking. But she'd had a sticker price a year ago when she upped the ante and married him into the bargain.

He hiked a devilish eyebrow. "My high priced investment I've yet to sample." He curled his lip, his words gliding off his tongue, both a threat and a promise. "But the feast begins now." Scooping her up in his arms, he strode across the living room and through the bedroom, booting the door shut.

****

Worth the wait. Cade yawned, shifting beneath the satin sheets of the king-size bed, the trite phrase streaking through his mind. A grin played on his mouth. This woman he married had been worth the cost and more, and not just in cash. For the first time, he felt like he'd finally come home, here, anywhere and everywhere in her arms...in her heart.

A tremor skittered across his abs.

He wasn't ready to admit it aloud; there were still too many questions, things to resolve between them. He glanced at the bedside clock. Four-thirty a.m. They still had the remainder of the night.

He stretched his arm out to touch her, draw her near, but encountered empty space. A spasm slammed his gut. He flipped over and relief zapped through him. Wrapped in her silk robe, she sat curled up on the chair at the table, the night lamp casting a halo about her tousled hair. She pursed her mouth in concentration...the mouth he'd kissed, drunk from, wanted more from. Desire coursed through him, and his body reacted to the catalyst.

A knockout.

His little mouse had turned siren. His wife, his lover, his— Could she be his confidante?

In their rustic mountain abode in Cyprus, he'd felt like a king with her beside him, although he hadn't admitted it. A king who'd lost his kingdom and was about to reclaim it with her as his queen. He chuckled at his fanciful musings, and she glanced up from what she was reading.

"Come to bed, darlin'." Already going hard for her, he patted the space beside him and the sheet slid to his waist.

She didn't move, not even a flicker of an eyelash, and slammed him with her glassy-eyed stare. A bleat of sound from deep in her throat.

Not a good sign.

"Something wrong?"

No answer, just the crunch of paper between her fingers, obliterating what she read.

A cab horn blared from the street below and severed the silence. Neon lights wavered through the crack in the velvet curtains, and then disappeared.

Cade zoned in on the document in her hand and groaned.

Thunder rolled, a lightning bolt, and wind and rain battered the windows. Typical London weather, he thought, but even the storm couldn't distract from the category five hurricane that was about to blast him indoors.

She jumped up, smacking her hands on the table and trapping the file beneath her fingers.

He vaulted off the mattress, snatched up the sheet and secured it at his waist.

"Nina..."

Crash and burn, man.

No, no, no, the word drummed in his head. Not after last night… they'd come too far to let it be stolen by misconceptions. He took a step closer and stumbled, his bare feet tangling in the satin folds. Breathing fast and heavy, he braked in his tracks, his heart battering his chest. The sheet dragged at his ankles, and he felt out of control. Cornered. He didn't like it. But he had to say something, anything to ease the shock from her face.

"I can explain."

"You used me."

"Nope." He dropped the sheet, grabbed his jeans from the armchair, and shoved his legs through them, not bothering to secure the snap at his waist. "It's not how it—"

"You used me to get to him." Her eyes glazed over as if she were looking right through him. Her voice seemed to come from a distance, the icy tone ripping at his abs. She drew in a sharp breath, exhaled, and nodded as if making sense of it in her own mind.

Dangerous ground, man.

Cade narrowed his focus, studying her face, her every nuance. *Do something. Say something.*

"That's why you married me." She laughed, the brittle sound scouring his bare chest. "All that baloney—"

"Baloney?" He tried to inject a slight note of amusement, hoping it'd nick through her righteous wrath.

Not a blink of an eyelash, or a twitch of a nerve at the corner of her mouth.

"—about the three mil to save your corporation was a cover. A con. A front," she accused. "You wanted to get to him, and I became your decoy."

She blinked, and a flicker of uncertainty crossed her features. A splinter of hope zinged through him. But the bleak look in her eyes, the emptiness in her voice…the hopelessness doused it.

"As if all those years in exile weren't enough for him and moth—" Her voice cracked. She pressed her hand to her mouth, and he almost missed. "And me."

He rubbed a fist across the groove carved on his forehead. Unable to connect the dots of her tirade, frustration fizzed through his brain. Cade always could put a puzzle together.

Except when it came to her.

"You had me in your sights twenty-four seven," she rambled, and he let her, thinking he might catch a clue to fit the pieces in sync. In a few hours, he'd have his answers from the VIP, his uncle. He smirked. He suspected his uncle had controlled the situation from the get go, and Cade had a hunch he hadn't been alone. His lungs compressed, then he inhaled, filling his chest with oxygen. Soon, he'd know the who and the why.

A gust of air shot from his mouth. Right now, he had to shake Nina from her self-inflicted trance and spark some color in her face.

He reached for her.

"Don't touch me." Nina shriveled away from him and collapsed on the chair, tucking her legs beneath her.

"Okay." He raised his hands above his head, his biceps bulging, and his eyes drilling into hers.

"Okay?" Nina squinted at him, her heart hammering and her body betraying her mind.

Barefoot, he stood tall with his jeans gaping open at the waist, his sex pressing against the half open zipper. She gulped. God help her. She still wanted him, wanted to—but she balled the paper in her hand and snapped out of it. "How could anything be okay, when you've been hunting m-my father?"

"Your father?"

She leaped from the chair and hurled the paper missile disclosing the damning evidence at him. "You had me investigated, you plotted," –she swept up the file, pointing it at him— "you schemed to use me to—to—destroy him."

"I didn't know he was your fath—"

All of a sudden the fight went out of her, and she slumped back in the chair, tears stinging her eyelids. But she would not give him the satisfaction of weeping in front of him.

"Nina, you have to listen." He jammed his fingers through his hair, pacing to and fro, finally stopping within a foot of her. "If I'm guilty, then you're right there with me for having done the same. Maybe worse."

She lifted her head, her eyes empty. "Wha-at?"

"You hooked me, pilfered my money, and jetted to Florence until you located him." He snapped his fingers, the puzzle locking into place. "You thought he was there, that's why you stole away the morning after our wedding." His lip curled. "You had your own agenda."

Her sharp intake of breath, a cyclone ripping between them.

"Your excuse for jumping ship?" He guffawed. "Eavesdropping—on my phone call to—"

"No." The one word a whiz of sound from her mouth. She gripped the chair's arms so hard, her knuckles whitened, and words snagged in her throat.

"Overheard—more palatable to you?" He shrugged, his shoulder blades tensing. "My negotiating the sale of one of Century's yachts." A pause, and his words crackled with scorn. "When your…er…father, wasn't in Florence, the boutique became your cover." A gale blasted from his mouth, whipping her face. "Cyprus became a pleasant—"

"For whom?"

"—if unexpected diversion," he continued like she hadn't spoken, and that had her fuming. "My euros financed your search and kept you in style until I tracked you down."

"I said I'd pay you back."

A pulsing beat, and—

"Then come back to bed."

A split second of silence, deep and foreboding.

Deliberately, she pushed up from the chair and took a step, the crack of her hand across his cheek vibrating between them.

He drew in a force of sound, his features taut...unyielding.

She swallowed, and licked her lips.

He flicked a glance from her mouth to the gaping neckline of her robe, outlining the swell of her breasts. A chuckle skidded from his throat, frosting her skin and shooting shards of ice into her spine. She clutched the lapels of her robe tight and dismissed the hardening of her nipples as mere reaction to the cold, and not his expression.

"Still denying?"

"No, I mean...it's not that simple."

"Well, sweetheart, nothing ever is." He stroked his knuckles across his cheek still stinging from her slap.

"I-I'm sorry—"

"Save it," he muttered, turning away. "I'm going to take a cold shower and by the time I'm done, be packed."

"Cade..."

He paused in stride, but didn't look her way. "Yeah?"

"It's not him," she murmured, her voice barely audible, shaky. "It's not my father who's—"

He nodded and yanked the door to the en-suite open.

"You know?" she asked, astounded. "Then why...who?"

"When we get to New York, the 'who' will surface," he hurled over his shoulder.

"But I don't want to go with you."

He spun around. "If you don't want your father named an accomplice in a global wide electronic scam, you'd better be ready to board Century One at twelve hundred hours."

"B-b-ut you said you knew it wasn't him."

"No, you said it," he clipped out.

"I-I don't understand."

Cade twisted his mouth in wry cynicism. "As you said, it's not that simple." His gut signaled her father wasn't as innocent as she seemed to think, but he couldn't explain now. But he bet his uncle held the deck, her father cut the cards and one other dealt the hand, working the ETF system. That's whom he had to nab to staunch the financial bleeding of Century Corporation.

He sized her up and down, and his body throbbed…for her.
Ruthlessly, he resisted the sexual pull to gather her up in his arms,
but her forlorn look penetrated his blockade, stabbing his heart.
Yeah, he'd get the hacker, but would it cost him Nina?

CHAPTER TEN

Cade stood with his hands behind his back, the brooding look in his eyes reflected in the wide expanse of window of his New York headquarters on Madison Avenue. The memory of their sexual tryst last night in his penthouse had him hardening up…but something else prodded his heart. Elusive. He couldn't identify it. And it was stoking his frustration. An epithet blasted from his mouth and tainted the air.

"Having a bad day already, dear?" Nina waltzed into his office, and stood her ground several feet from him, his surprise at her appearance evident from his face. She glanced over her shoulder at her old office…a bittersweet memory taunted, and her back went rigid. "Your receptionist must've gone on a loo break, so I showed myself in."

He nodded, taciturn.

"My debt's paid in full." She tossed the penthouse keys on his desk, taking in every flicker of his face; the flare of his nose, the shuttering of his eyes, the set of his mouth. Her pulse skittered and her palms went damp. Images replayed in her mind…him holding her, touching, tasting…heaven. Emotion rose inside her, and she clutched her handbag, willing herself to breathe normally.

"How do you figure that?"

"The deal was for one night…" She couldn't get the word 'sex' out. It sounded so cold, mechanical, impersonal; and there had been nothing cold or clinical about their lovemaking. It had been a volcanic eruption of the senses and the heart…at least for her.

"With me."

She nodded, wanting more…of him. But she couldn't, not without his love. It would crush her. Be strong, be smart, she told herself. A wisp of a smile. Smarter.

"Yes." It had been a memorable night of passion with him. Unforgettable. A knife twisted in her heart. "And now it's done… it's over."

Shifting a step, she had the armchair between them. He noted her movement, and his eyes turned glacial. She gripped the smooth leather to steady her jelly-filled legs.

Mere hours ago, Nina had fluttered her eyelashes and with a satisfied smile on her face, stretched across the king-size bed to touch him. Her hand landed on the empty pillow, her eyes flew open, and fuzz filled her brain cells. She had squinted at the note propped on the bedside table lamp, and her heart plummeted to her pink-tipped toes curling on the satin sheet. His scent, cool spice and man, clung to the sheets, spiking her memory with every detail of their sizzling night.

A bleat of sound slipped from her mouth, exploded in a groan, and even the New York traffic far below couldn't smother the hopelessness of it.

An image of their village abode flashed through her mind, and the groan morphed into a wistful sigh. It'd been rough, he'd been demanding and bossy, and sparks had flown—but oddly enough, she'd been happy in a simple, uncomplicated way.

She snatched the note, and his impersonal words scrawled in black ink, smacked her face. *'Returning late. Chauffeur at your disposal.'* C.S.

A shiver ran through her, and her teeth chattered. She drew the sheet closer about her and huddled beneath. He hadn't even signed the thing.

In the lull of her thoughts, her heart thumped her ribs. One, two, three…she chided herself at her idiocy. What did she expect? A declaration of love? An epiphany after one night with her? She laughed, and the sound turned to a whimper.

She might be married to him, but she was no wife to him, not even for one night. A one-time mistress would be more like it. She turned up her nose and sniffed. A mistress might fare better than she had under his controlling dictates. She pressed her eyelashes closed, determined not to cry, but her lip quivered. She wanted to scream, to release her anger at him and at her own foolishness.

A tear oozed beneath her lashes, slid down her cheek and settled on the corner of her mouth. She flicked it away with her tongue, the saltiness stinging the bleakness inside her. She hiccupped and hugged his pillow. Another tear welled up and spilled over, then another.

Finally, she sucked in mouthfuls of oxygen and knew what she had to do. Must do. For her sanity, for her father, for her business in Florence, before everything she'd worked for bit the dust. She managed to drag herself from the bed and to the shower.

She dressed in a classic Chanel suit and stilettos to boost her confidence. After applying a touch of mascara and lipstick, she swept her hair up in a chignon, clipped gold hoops in her ears and packed her few belongings. She flirted with the idea of skipping out while he was at work but that'd be cowardly. For her dignity and peace of mind, she had to see him. Confront him one more time.

"Paid in full." She enunciated each word, hoping that hearing them again would convince her.

A silent beat.

"You've paid a portion," he said, his tone unflinching.

Startled, she gaped at him. "What?"

Cade tried to crush the erotic kick in his male counterparts, but it didn't work. He wanted her…more nights with her…a lifetime of sensual delight. Their passion blasted all records—his chest expanded, his blood heated—images of her with him, under him,…skyrocketing…flashed through his psyche.

"A night is what we agreed on." He shoved his hands in his jeans' pockets, and drew closer.

She inched backward but the edge of his desk stopped her.

Good.

"A night—half of a twenty-four cycle—twelve hours." He cleared his throat. "A technicality" –he shrugged— "but since we got a late start" –his eyes bore into her, into her soul to extract something, anything that'd give him the edge— "our midnight madness lasted say two hours—"

She averted her gaze, so he couldn't decipher her reaction.

So, he went on full throttle— "add our one hour pre-dawn frolic in the Jacuzzi…"

Her face flamed.

"…tops, three hours." Another step brought him within inches of her, her exotic perfume ensnared, and he closed the gap. "The electrical combustion afterward would be another two."

Was that a catch in her breath? Or his?

"Total, five hours…with you," he murmured, his words gruffer than he intended. "If not for the emergency at the site this morning and the pending VIP meet in an hour, we'd still be—"

"London?" she whispered, her voice wavering.

"Moot point." He brushed stray tendrils at her nape with his knuckles, tempted to bury his face in the softness. "You didn't come back to bed."

Lifting a few strands, he brushed the ends across his mouth, then allowed them to drift between his fingers. Silky, smooth, sensual. "You still owe me seven hours…in my bed."

"You can't be serious." She licked her lips, and that had his gut clenching. Then, she turned her baby blues full force on him and sucker-punched him in the solar plexus.

And because of that, his tone grew harsher. "I am…serious."

"You're unreasonable."

"You will pay my due to the last minute, second—"

"Your heart's made of stone."

Her words nearly felled him, but he remained resolute. His uncle's morning text warned something big was going down tonight. Cade had to keep her under surveillance to ensure she didn't wander into a danger zone.

"You will do as I say."

"If I refuse?" Her chin went up a notch.

"You'll have to pay the balance in cold hard cash."

"You know I don't have that kind of money." The obstinate angle of her chin softened, and her lashes fluttered, shielding her eyes, but her tone remained cool…all business.

He shrugged. "Then you had better warm my bed tonight."

"No."

"I wouldn't be so hasty." His words were smooth steel. "Papa might get caught in the crossfire."

Her head snapped around.

He lifted a sardonic brow.

"Cade, no," she pleaded.

"I'll see you tonight."

She didn't move, setting off her own flare. "I'll call him."

A pause, then— "Go ahead."

Squinting at him, she pulled her cell from her purse and keyed in the number, her hand quivering. Seconds ticked by, and she caught her lip between her teeth, her cheeks going pale.

"Something wrong?" he asked, sotto voce.

"The subscriber's number is not in service," she mumbled, dazed. "But he always answers my calls."

"Apparently not today." He propped his hip on the edge of the desk, rolled up his sleeves, his covert gaze playing tug-of-war with hers.

Unaware of her effect on him, she licked lip-gloss from her bottom lip, her luminous eyes glazing over. He had a gut-checking moment.

Civility was not all it was cut out to be.

He wanted to swat everything off the desk and take her on the glossy top. Every muscle in his torso corded, and he crunched down on his molars.

No interference. Not even Nina. From nabbing the bad man and stemming the financial gutting of his corporation. Tonight.

"Where is he?" she accused, her fists pounding his chest. "What have you done with my father?"

"Hey," he muttered, grabbing her wrists. "I'm a businessman, not a monster."

"That's debatable." She pulled away from him, her body language reflecting her resentment, and he let go so quickly, she stumbled back into a chair.

"Call him tomorrow, Nina."

"Why?"

He tilted his mouth in a cocky grin. "By tomorrow you'll be all paid up, honey."

A sharp intake of breath, and she spun around to leave, but he shifted, blocking her path.

"Tuh, tuh." He propelled her against him, swooped down and claimed her mouth with his. A heartbeat later, he released her. "A taste of what's to come, darlin'."

"You're a bast—"

He pressed the intercom, his words cold…cruel. "Mrs. Sloan is leaving. Send in my next appointment."

Nina rushed out of the office, her eyes blurring with tears and bumped into the blonde receptionist strolling back in. She kept her finger on the elevator button, willing it to hurry up.

"Mr. Sloan said you forgot your keys." The receptionist poked her head back out of the door, dangling the keys from her fingers and fluffing her short bob with her other hand.

"I have another set, thanks." *But not to the penthouse*, the thought zipped across her mind.

At that moment, the elevator doors slid open, and Nina slipped inside, relieved. The elevator closed and began its descent. Mr. Big and Mighty Sloan was coming in for a crash landing. She still had an ace to play. But, first she'd ensure her father was safe by calling the only other person he'd confide in.

Nina hurried across the lobby to the restroom and retrieved the Macy's shopping bag she'd stashed in the nook behind the trashcan earlier. She left behind everything he'd given her—gowns, jewelry, shoes. A wry smile teased her mouth. Her favorite Italian shoes had been a temptation, but she'd learned her lesson. She'd owe him nothing more.

In order not to alert his chauffeur, she'd stuffed her few belongings in a shopping bag, rather than a suitcase. Clutching the bag in her hand, she hurried across the foyer, her heels clicking on the marble tiles. The moment she stepped through the revolving doors, she got bumped into the stream of humanity.

Clouds loomed overhead.

The pretzel man stood on one street corner, the hot dog stand opposite, the pita & falafel seller rolled his trolley along the sidewalk, the T-shirt vendor and the flower girl claimed their own spots to the backdrop of beeping yellow cabs—a unique trademark of the New York weave.

Nina flagged down a cab, and when it swerved to a stop, she tossed the bag in the back and followed it. "John F. Kennedy Airport, please."

A squeal of tires, and the cabby barged into the flow of traffic; passing a Starbucks spilling over with patrons on a coffee fix prior to boarding the subway, and whizzing past Patrick leaning against the parked limo.

She twisted around, and a grin curved her mouth. The chauffeur tugged off his cap, tossed it on the ground, snatched it up, and dove into the limo; nosing away from the curb after her.

A giggle bubbled in her throat, and she leaned back against the seat, closing her eyes. Reprieve. Cade's chauffeur would never catch up to her through the morning rush hour.

A sobering thought flashed through her mind and the giggle dissipated. She hooked a loose curl behind her ear, her heart hammering and her hands clammy.

What would happen when Cade caught up with her?

There would be hell to pay.

CHAPTER ELEVEN

"She gave you the slip?" Cade vaulted from his chair and pressed the intercom. "Cancel all my appointments."

He swept up his Armani overcoat and sprinted for the elevator, barking orders into his cell, barely noticing his secretary's open-mouthed confusion. "On my way down…Waldorf…quickest route."

A hush, and the elevator doors slid open. He stepped inside, disconnected the call to his chauffeur and pressed the line to his pilot. "Prepare the Lear for take-off." He glanced at the Omega on his wrist. "I'll be at Kennedy within the hour."

******

Patrick pulled the limo to a stop in front of the Waldorf-Astoria and Cade leaped out, storming through the Park Avenue entrance.

"Uhm…dress code." The bellman ogled Cade's mud-caked boots beneath his Armani coat. Cade gave him a fierce look. The man stepped aside, and he crossed the chandelier-lit lobby.

Cade barged into Sir Harry's bar, scanned the dim interior and grimaced. Struck out again. His uncle and Nina's father—no shows. A growl of frustration erupted from deep in his chest. He spun around to exit and bumped into a woman rushing in.

"I-I'm glad I got here in time," she said, anxiety cracking her words.

"Sorry, you've got the wrong guy." He sidestepped her. What a pick-up line.

"I don't…" She grabbed his arm. "…have the wrong guy."

"Lady—" He braked to a stop, noted the concern in her features…her eyes. Memory knocked, and he snapped his fingers. "Limassol Wine Fest…my uncle's date."

"Actually," she murmured, wringing her gloved hands, "I'm his wife and—"

"You have a message from him?" Cade demanded, his words crackling with impatience.

She gave him a level look with her mascara-fringed eyes that made him squirm. And Cade Sloan never, but *never*, squirmed, not since he was a kid of six. Her hazel irises reflected a ring of gold—golden-brown eyes.

Like his own.

Shock immobilized him for a second, and then feelings he'd buried deep inside him for almost thirty years erupted in an avalanche of bitterness. It must've reflected on his face, for she closed the gap with a step and reached for him.

He shook his head and backtracked a couple of paces; then his discipline kicked in, and he stood his ground. Nothing made sense. Was everyone mad? Or just him?

"I can explain," she murmured, almost pleading.

"You had better." Cade took her elbow, guiding her to a secluded table in the corner and nodded to the bartender. He needed a drink. Strong, black coffee. And by the peaked look on her face, she did too, spiked with something stronger. "You have exactly ten minutes."

"I can do it in five," she blurted. "Details, I'll leave for another time."

"Get started." He plunked down in the chair opposite, giving her no quarter.

At the close of her tale, stunned, Cade pushed his untouched coffee aside and stood up to leave.

"Easy there." A man dug his fingers in his shoulder and shoved him back down.

"What—" Cade sank in the chair, the point of the gun digging in his ribs. Fine hair on the back of his head stood on end…there was something familiar about the gunman. Acrid taste scoured his tongue. "Daddy Sloan?" His nickname for his father slipped out unconsciously from Cade's lips.

"Long time no see," the stranger blustered, concealing the firearm beneath his coat.

"No." His mother rose to her feet, her face ashen.

"You got that right, lil' lady," he blurted, his alcohol laden breath tainting the air. "Your pre-wedding fling with the favorite son popped this bastard, but I wasn't fooled."

Cade siphoned a gallon of air into his lungs, and then let it hiss between his teeth, every sinew in his body primed for attack. "You…uh… missed me and decided to come calling?"

His father shot him a furious look, and ignored his wisecrack.

"Joe always had the upper hand over half-bro here, but I got you anyway," he bragged, his eyes shifty. "Willingly or not."

"But you didn't keep me," his mother murmured.

"Shut up," the gunman ordered, and then guffawed. "I slammed you Sloans where it hurt most, your bank account." He grabbed Cade's untouched coffee, poured it down his throat and swiped his mouth with the back of his hand. "He laughs best who laughs last."

"What is it you want?" Cade demanded, the irony smashing him between the eyes. The man he chased for over a year stood inches from him, and he couldn't make a move to bring him down.

"Do as I say and no one gets hurt." His father motioned them to get moving, his hand in his coat pocket, his signal clear. "A ride to Sloan…er… Century Global for a final transaction, and we'll call it a day." A pause… "And that lil' lady you've been sporting on your arm will be off the hook."

"Nina." Cade breathed her name on an intake of breath. "If you've touched her I'll break you apart."

"You're hardly in a position to call the shots." And to emphasize his point, he nudged him with the revolver. "Excuse the pun," he chortled. "Now step on it."

Cade thought he must be in a parallel universe…past and present about to detonate. Stuck in the middle, he racked his brains for a way to douse the fuse, and then chuckled. "Nothing quick about battling New York rush hour traffic."

That hit a nerve, and the enemy's face folded in distaste, his mouth a thin line. "Radio for the chopper…and no tricks."

"No."

He grabbed his mother and pressed the weapon into her back. "Gimme another answer, boy."

"Yes," Cade amended on a heartbeat, meeting his mother's terror-stricken eyes. He pulled out his cell phone, uttered an order, and clicked off. "This way."

"I give the orders," his father boasted, chewing his bottom lip.

Cade inclined his head in acquiescence, and Daddy Sloan paused, inspecting the door exit to East 50th Street. "Outside. We'll climb the fire escape to the roof."

The moment they set foot on the pavement, two NYPD vehicles screeched to a stop and blocked their path, sirens ripping through the air. "Drop it and raise your hands." The officers leaped out, took cover behind the cars and drew their pistols.

Panicked, his father grabbed his mother and using her as a human shield, dragged her with him to the deserted parking structure.

A police chopper circled overhead.

He shoved her at the officers and made a run for it.

Cade sprinted after him and tackled, the gun hurling from his hand and skidding across the asphalt. A brief scuffle, and Cade yanked him up by the collar. "Hands over your head…Daddy Sloan." Cade shoved him forward into the officers' hands. "Your visit's been cut short."

A third cop car swerved in. His uncle and Nina's father shuffled from the back seat, and Cade grinned. "A family affair."

"Not exactly," his mother murmured from the shadows.

Cade snapped his head her way, but didn't move.

"He's not your father," his mother blurted, her features riddled in shock.

"Any more surprises?" Cade muttered, noting his uncle securing an arm around her shoulders. Heck, he felt like a tidal wave had upended him, and then a nuclear blast scrambled his brain. He got it, but a part of him resisted. A myriad of emotions pummeled his insides, turning his words rough. "Someone better tell me what the heck's going on."

"I will," Nina's father said, stepping up to the plate.

"Where's Nina?" Cade snarled.

"On her way to Florence."

"How do you know?"

"She called her mother, trying to reach me."

Grim-faced, Cade nodded, relief spreading through him. She was safe.

"We'll fill you in on the way to the airport." His uncle clamped a hand on his shoulder, and his muscles knotted. "I've got my lady, now go get yours...son."

"I intend to," Cade bit out in force. But could he?

******

Cade felt like a bull in a china shop, standing smack center on the shop floor of the Fantasy Secrets boutique. Shoving back his hardhat, he curved his mouth in a lopsided grin and perused the merchandise.

No sign of Nina.

He flicked his fingers across a scarlet satin chemise draped over a mannequin, the sensual feel reminding him...of her. Demolishing the smile from his mouth, he dismissed the frilly nothings surrounding him and trekked to the counter.

97

Several weeks had elapsed before Cade could extricate himself from the legalities in New York, and jet to Florence. After he arrived, still trying to make sense of the bombshell his mother and uncle…er …father had detonated in his life, he hadn't sought Nina out immediately.

A self-deprecating grunt echoed from deep in his throat. Today, after touring the development now designed to rebuild rather than bulldoze, he knew the time had come to confront his runaway Cinderella.

He pressed the buzzer next to the computerized cash register.

Swiping his palm across his dirt-stained jeans, he heaved a breath. His gut whipped. Absurd. He was the CEO of Century Corporation, grossing millions globally—that was assured now profits stayed within the company—and here he was feeling like a nerdy teen on his first date. And just because of that, he tautened his features and banged the bell.

Silence.

He palmed the bell again, the sound reverberating around the shop.

"We're closed," she called from somewhere in back, her words muffled. "Didn't you see the closed shutters?"

The sound of her voice was smooth as Southern Comfort on a wintry night, it washed over him, stimulating every fiber of his body.

He kept his finger on the buzzer.

"Who—" She hurled from behind the curtained partition, and lurched to a stop, her eyes wide with surprise, or was that shock? Removing the pins clamped between her teeth, she poked them in the negligee draped over her arm and brushed the bangs off her forehead. Her elusive scent floated to him, distinguishable even amidst the bottled fragrances and scented candles on the shelves. She'd turned out to be as indefinable as the perfume she wore… and just as provocative.

Sensual.

Sexy.

She tilted her chin and lowered her lashes, her eyes blue slits.

"Wha-at are you do—we're closed," she said, her mouth set.

A jab that hit the mark…right beneath his heart, and he almost vaulted the counter to steal a kiss…kisses. His Adam's apple bopped, and he flexed his abs, controlling his ardor.

"Nope." He tucked the work-hat under his arm and inclined his head to the door. "Sign says five-thirty." A glance at his wrist, and he rapped the watch with his knuckle. "Two more minutes."

"Very well." She sighed and turning her back to him, hung up the snowy fluff of nothing on a rack. Dawdling, she removed the pins, fiddled with the price tag and smoothed the folds.

He hooked his boot on the rung of a stool, his jaw taut.

Finally, she spun around, her features tense, her eyes glinting ice. "What can I do for you?"

"Naa, naa." He wiggled his brows and planted his boot back on the floor. "It's what I can do for you."

"Really?" She elevated a shapely eyebrow. "What might that be?"

He grinned.

Her brow dropped back in place, and she assessed him suspiciously.

"I want to buy a gift for a special lady," he said, his gaze clashing with hers. "And the woman I love."

"Certainly." She hurled the word at him like a snowball, her voice an Arctic breeze.

He frowned. Was there a skid beneath her self-assured demeanor? Good. Perhaps his words had drilled through the frosty exterior to prick her heart. She certainly had nailed tacks into his.

"I hope you find what you want."

"Me, too." He drummed his fingers on the counter.

That garnered him another glare. "What did you have in mind?"

Oh, baby, if you knew what was in my mind. "Uh…something hot, sexy." His eyes never left her face, and then his grin broadened. "Like the one there. On the rack behind you."

"It's very expensive."

"She's worth it."

She nearly gagged at that and clearing her throat, found her voice. "Size?"

He tilted his head, pursed his lips and measured with his hands in the air. "About yours."

"Pardon?"

"Your size should fit her just fine."

"Of course." She spanned her hands on the counter, whizzing in a breath, and he noted the wedding ring still on her finger. A Tarzan yell exploded inside him, but he kept his game face on, tuning into her words.

"Our exclusive lingerie is made to fit all shapes and sizes."

"I'll take it."

Another Arctic front blasted, depositing another layer of frost between them.

"That'll be thirteen thousand euros."

"A real bargain," he mocked.

"We do an exceptional job."

"I'm expecting it." He winked.

Nina flicked a curl off her shoulder, her pulse all a flutter again.

The rogue. The blackguard. The jerk. She gritted her teeth, running out of choice adjectives to hurl at him, even if it was only in her mind. He'd stolen her heart with his *laissez-faire* attitude and then, stomped on it. Why else would he be buying gifts for another woman? Well, she wouldn't let him know how much it got to her.

"We aim to please our customers," she murmured, giving him a coquettish smile.

"Yeah," he ground out, his mouth firm.

"Will that be cash or credit?" Nina removed the negligee from the hanger, allowing the sheer silk trimmed with fur to slide between her fingers. "No personal checks. No exceptions."

He raised both eyebrows, and then slammed them back in place, entrapping her in his laser-sharp focus for a long hot beat. "Natch." Shrugging, he pulled out his wallet from the back pocket of his jeans.

"Would you like it gift wrapped?" She took a gift box from beneath the counter, set it on top and outlined it with gold speckled tissue paper.

"Not before I see it in action."

"What do you mean?" She picked up a pair of scissors from the shelf, snipped off a length of ribbon from the roll, replaced the shears and folded the garment. Had to keep busy, the mantra drummed in her head, and remain detached from his sexual magnetism. Fat chance, but she had to try, didn't she?

"Surely a demo job goes with that rip-off price?" He slid a finger down the bridge of his nose, and pursed his mouth.

Her hands stilled over the folds of the fabric, and she rammed him with a glassy stare. Was that a shadow of tenderness in his eyes? It couldn't be for her. It was either that or a trick of the twilight glowing behind the sealed shutters.

"A demo—what?"

"You know, model it."

"Sorry, the model has left for the day."

"You'll do."

"No."

"Scared?"

"No private showings without security present." Her words were barbed, and she hoped she hit the mark…right into his heart. "And none to strangers."

He winced, but quickly rebounded. "I'm no stranger." He green-lighted her head to toe with his gaze, spot-checking her cleavage, the apex of her thighs and back up to her mouth, her eyes.

Her stomach plummeted, and then righted, her nerves twittered, but she managed to toss him a haughty look. "That could be disputed."

A smirk, and he chuckled. "Not from where I'm standing."

"What is it you want, Cade?"

"To spend money on my lady." He pulled out a wad of bills from his wallet, tossed them on the counter, and then shoved the wallet in his back pocket. "Throw that red number on my tab too. A wedding gift."

Nina gripped the counter with one hand and squashed gold ribbon with the other. The hotshot from Manhattan had returned in full form on Roman soil; swinging in the groove and brandishing his wealth on gifts for his new *amour*. And already talking about another nuptial hook up.

A bitter taste scoured her throat, her heart, and her emotions. She had been foolish to entertain even the remotest possibility that he'd come for her...come to work things out.

A dry sound whisked from her mouth.

"Something amusing?"

"Ye...no." No way would she strut before him in that x-rated froth of fabric simply for his joy ride. The padlock around her heart clicked in place. It hurt. Too much.

He'd seen her in less, touched her everywhere, kissed, fondled... She didn't want to remember, but her body thrummed with awareness. A silent moan spread through her, every cell vibrating to alertness...desire.

"Shall I call *my* security, Nina?"

"No need," she said, her tone dismissive. "You can take your business elsewhere."

"Can't."

"Why not?"

"Stores are closed, remember?"

"Not my problem."

"Could be?"

"How so?"

"Had a talk with your father."

She laughed. "You can't play that card on me again, Cade. I talked with him too."

"And?" He caught her in his hawkish sights, challenging... assessing.

Her lashes dipped. "He explained about your father...your uncle...not..." Her words trailed off, her tone softening, and she lifted her lashes, giving him a direct look.

"Yeah, well," Cade grunted. "I'm a big boy."

A tense silence fractured only by the sound of traffic along the Via Cassia, the main route south to Rome.

"I'll...uh...have this wrapped up for you in a sec," she murmured.

He propped his elbows on the counter and leaned forward, so closely she could smell his aftershave...cool spice...mingled with sweat and man. It brought back all the memories she had tried to forget.

Erotic.

Sensual. Arousing.

Maddening.

"Then you don't know?" he said, his tone confidential, his breath tickling her cheek.

"Know what?" She snapped away from her thoughts, her hands hovering over the negligee.

A wolfish smile slashed his mouth. "You play and I'll say."

"What?"

"Model it."

"Blackmail, Cade?"

He grinned. "Never."

She slapped her hands on the counter, and her bracelet jiggled. "I want to know what it is first."

"Go change, and I'll spice up the conversation."

"You first."

He rubbed the back of his neck with his hand and pushed away from the counter. "Your father and my uncle hatched a—"

"Go on."

"Uh, uh." He motioned her to the fitting room. "Your move."

How dare he come in here, buying sexy gifts for—well she wouldn't dwell on that—and if that hadn't been enough, demanding she play pinup girl and spinning some tale of intrigue to trip her up. A hissy fit was in the making, but she squashed that inclination, deciding instead to teach him a lesson he wouldn't soon forget.

"Well, okay." She swept her hair to one side, her earring jangling and turned her back. "Unzip me, please."

Or would she get burned in the process?

"Careful, it might get stuck."

"Sure thing." Cade stepped closer, tempted to bend his head and nuzzle her neck, feasting on her pulse point. *Don't rush it.* He tautened his torso, crushed the craving but couldn't resist brushing the stray curls from her nape. He lowered the zipper until his fingers skimmed the dip of her back, itching to explore further. A blast of air from his mouth, and he curved his palm on her hip.

"Did it catch?" she whispered, denting his already tenuous control.

She shifted in his hands, and he wanted to take, hold—

"Naa." He checked the alluring curves of her derriere and just when he made up his mind to touch, stroke, cup, she turned around in his arms.

"Thank you." She tilted her head his way, her voice husky, her lashes shadowing her eyes.

His gut coiled. Had he just lost command of the situation? This five-foot-two with eyes that could turn to midnight with passion and glitter ice blue with annoyance had in the last two minutes gotten the upper hand. And he didn't like it, not at all.

"Sure, anytime."

She swept up the negligee and trotted to the fitting room, tossing over her shoulder. "Continue."

Hmm, playing games was she? He'd go along and see where it got him.

"My father and your uncle plotted…" she prompted, her voice catching.

"To get us hitched."

She jerked to a stop, her back stiffening, her hands squeezing the silk. "They conspired to get us— why?"

"To protect—"

She spun around. "Who?"

He inclined his head toward the changing room.

She scurried inside.

"You."

"Protect me?" She poked her head out from behind the curtain.

"Why? From what? Whom?"

He shook his index finger at her. "Tuh, tuh."

She quickly withdrew, the dress slid to her ankles and she stepped from it.

"Married to me, you'd have legal claim to Century Corp." He glimpsed her feet from beneath the drapes, the graceful arch of her instep, her— *Focus, man.* "Securing your financial future— a payoff for your father's lifetime of service. And" –he paused, debated— "A sleight of hand against the hacker."

"Really?" she queried, the word muffled by the swish of cloth behind the curtain.

"Sheltering a portion of Century's assets—"

"In my name," she said, her words clearer now.

"—in the event the hacker gutted the company before we could spring him with the goods."

"You mean I own half of Century Corp?"

"Not exactly," he grunted. "When you ditched, the backer… backers scrambled to revise their plan."

"Your uncle…real father—"

"And yours."

"I see." But did she? Nina slipped the sheer fabric over her head, wiggled and it fell, a soft caress upon her breasts and barely covering her tush. "And now?"

"It's over."

She didn't have to wonder if his words carried a double meaning. She brushed her hands over her hips, the sensual feel of silk an answer. But it was for another woman. A sour taste skimmed her tongue, tainting her words.

"Let's see," she murmured, more to herself than to him. "About to tank, you sold out for three mil and a stint at matrimony."

"A strategic move, Nina," he said, impatience in his voice. "In a dire financial clinch."

"Not your usual M.O," she mocked. Any way she looked at it, she'd been played. By Cade, his uncle and her father. "I became your collateral, in case things collapsed."

"It was a protective device, okay."

"For whom?" she sniped back.

"I told you," he bit back. "You."

"How chivalrous." Sarcasm dripped from her words. "A defunct company is useless."

"Okay, and me," he barked. "At the time I hadn't realized uncle… er…dad, was on my side." He paced the floor outside her dressing room.

"When I first began work at Sloan Global—"

"You tagged Century—"

"Yeah." He scrubbed a hand across his face.

"Your uncle—" she prompted, wanting to wrap her arms around him, comfort him.

"Hedged me from the company, taking the brunt of the scandal, and I almost annihilated him." His words ripped from him in a harsh sound. "At the Limassol Wine Fest I refused his help and almost sabotaged the sting."

"A little hard-headed are you, Cade?" she mouthed the rhetorical question more to herself than to him.

"Is that what you call it?" he shot back, sounding ticked off that she even voiced it.

She grinned. Served him right. "Anything else I should know?"

He chuckled at the double entendre of her words. "To disrupt the hacker's op, the IT—"

"My father."

"And my uncle tapped funds from Century…a trickle at a time, into your secured account."

"And I had no idea," she said with glee, peering at him through the crack in the curtain. "I am a major shareholder of Century Corp."

"Pocket change," he said, his mouth lifting at the corner. "Enough for a couple of pairs of those designer shoes you're crazy about."

"You noticed?"

"It's my job to notice things."

Her heart sank. There he went, lumping her with his other work obligations. "How good of you." Acid dabbed her words.

"Isn't it?" His comeback dipped in sarcasm. "Anyway, to wrap this up—"

"Yes, let's be done with it."

His eyes narrowed, a deafening pause and, "We got him."

She took another peek at him between the drapes, and her pulse faltered. Towering above the mannequins, he stood with legs astride, hooked a thumb at the fastening of his jeans, and propped the hardhat on his hip. His half open shirt revealed the sprinkle of hair on his chest, and she longed to touch him.

The man oozed sexual charisma.

A lock of hair flopped over his brow, and she wanted to step out and smooth it away. Of course, she didn't move an inch. She had to combat his magnetic pull with a cool retort. "You had no inkling of your uncle's and my father's reversed Electronic Transfer Fund conspiracy?"

"Not 'til it was almost a *fait accompli*." He shoved his rolled up sleeves higher on his arms, the muscles of his forearms flexing. "It took some fancy footwork to keep the company afloat."

She pressed a hand to her mouth, muting a giggle bubbling inside her. Somehow she couldn't see Cade doing a jig to anyone's fiddle. "You expect me to believe that?"

"Yeah," he struck back.

"Why?"

"Because it's the truth."

"Huh." She slipped her feet into stiletto-heeled slippers and drew the curtain aside.

"Nina…" He drew in a sharp breath and gulped a grunt of sound.

Okay, she thought, pleased. His reaction at least soothed her pride, but not a moment later, he dashed it.

"An ingenious cyber sting," he said, nudging his chin with his fist. "The hacker snared at his own ETF game."

"A real soap opera," Nina said, tongue-in-cheek.

"My uncle had gotten the company and the girl—"

"Your mom," Nina murmured, brushing the fur trim of the negligee.

A curt nod from Cade. "As runner up, 'Daddy' Sloan felt thwarted and set out to cause damage where he could."

"And your uncle had no idea his half-bro forced your mother into marriage, then punished her by taking you away from her?"

"Pigheadedness runs in the family," Cade muttered, but his mouth curved in a reluctant grin. "Once clued in, uncle stepped up his visits to London until he got her away from him." Cade's features turned fierce. "But it was no cake walk. 'Daddy' Sloan had an ace up his sleeve."

Nina walked toward him, the swish of silk against her thighs a seductive sound. About to touch his arm, she stayed the motion and opened her eyes wide. Realization smacked her brain. "Oh my gosh, his ace was you…his next target."

Cade inclined his head in assent. "Bitterness led to booze and gambling, until his addiction took precedence over his vendetta." He rapped his hardhat with his knuckles. "His fix—an ongoing stream of cash. Sloan…Century…you," Nina murmured. "Became his supply."

He chuckled, a mirthless sound. "Quite astute, my dear."

Nina winced, the endearment having caught her off guard. To avoid analyzing it to smithereens and to cover the awkward moment, she slipped the scarlet satin chemise off the hanger.

"He banked no one would suspect a Sloan stealing from a Sloan," Cade added, a savage twist to his mouth. "It worked until the head of the tech department—"

"My father—"

"Caught him."

Nina tottered, grabbing onto the rack for support, her hand flying to her mouth, suddenly everything clear. "He was the one…he retaliated… spewed lies to my mom—threatened—" Her fingers fisted over the satin. "Silenced my father and shipped him off to Cyprus."

"Yeah," he muttered, the tense corners of his mouth easing a bit.

"What now?" she asked.

"All's well that—"

"Ends well."

"Shakespeare." They said in unison. But could that sage advice reflect on them?

Nina doubted it. Sounded more like a Romeo and Juliet curtain call.

"If your uncle had told you, none of this would've happened and you and I—" she broke off, swallowing the rest of her words.

"Would never have gotten hitched?" he clipped out, rolling his shoulders. "But we did."

She remained silent, stroking the satin with her fingertips, waiting… not sure of what. Maybe a signal from him that— she lifted her lashes and collided with his blade-thin focus.

"Now that I've reconciled my past," he said, "it's time I took care of my future."

She held her breath and her heart tripped. Obviously, he considered her in his past, otherwise, why was he buying gifts for another woman?

"I'll collect on what I paid for."

"Of course." She had no illusions. With every cell in her body splintering, she hurled the words at him. "After the show, I'll sign."

"Sign what?"

"The divorce documents."

A laser couldn't have sliced through the tension between them, but the police siren outside did.

"Let's have a little fun first, shall we?"

CHAPTER TWELVE

Nina shot him a look that could've frazzled toast to a crisp, but it didn't deter him, not one iota. And that had her hackles rising even more.

"Since it's costing me mega bucks—" he brushed his upper lip with his knuckle— "let's see that little number you're wearing in action."

Nina smashed down a groan pummeling her chest. He hadn't even given a hoot when she spoke of divorce; his cool indifference, a hailstorm assaulting her body. He wanted fun, did he? Well, she'd wallop him with it, but not at her expense. So, she did the only thing a savvy businesswoman would do.

"The modeling job will be an additional five hundred euros." Her frosty words snapped off her tongue, camouflaging her frayed emotions. "If you want the red on show" –she pointed to the satin with a more modest cut on the counter— "we have a special, two for nine hundred and ninety."

He curled his lip, and then chuckled. "The one you're wearing will do."

"Hot 'n sexy enough for you?" She flashed him a withering look beneath her lashes, but it didn't faze him.

He stroked the earring in his earlobe, his laser-sharp gaze drilling into her. "Depends who's wearing it."

His callous words pumped her indignation. How uncouth of him. Her temperature simmered and then flamed, melting the ice shackles around her heart. "In that case use your imagination."

"Don't have to."

She shrugged. "Please yourself."

"Oh, I intend to."

She did a double take, but his features remained unreadable, except for the tilt at the corner of his mouth, a cross between a smirk and a grin. "Well, then, make yourself comfortable, sir—"

Sir? Cade grumbled to himself. First she stole him blind with those padded prices, and now she shredded his ego, treating him like any jock off the street. That did not sit well with the Sloan pride. Seemed the lady might have her own agenda. Question was, where'd he fit on her list of priorities?

"—in the parlor." She waved him to an archway adjacent to the dressing room, her words silky soft.

Seductive.

A promise of things to come?

"Yeah, thanks." He rubbed a hand across his unshaven jaw and watched her walk away, hips swaying.

"I'll be with you in a moment," she said, her words whisper soft. A nerve bashed his cheek, and deleting it with his fist, he stomped to the boudoir and skidded to a halt. If he felt like a bull in the china shop earlier, he was now the fish out of water, surrounded by French provincial decor. Plush sofas curved around the mirrored walls, gold tussles dangling from the armrests and pink velvet cushions were strewn everywhere.

He glanced at the ceiling, caught his reflection tagged with building site marks, and grimaced. He should've changed, but he even nixed the closing of a multi-million dollar deal to catch her before she left.

A heave of a breath, and he strode across the thick carpet, plopping on the couch, the cushions dipping beneath his weight. He set his hardhat on the floor, and winced at the imprints his work boots left on the carpet. Another five hundred cleaning fee on his tab for sure.

The lights dimmed, the mirrorball began to spin and a seductive melody serenaded the room. He bolted to attention.

Show time.

Nina strutted in, veiled behind an ostrich-feather fan, her steps keeping tempo with the music, her body undulating. Flecks of light netted her hair, her skin, and glinted off the mirrors. A frown, and Cade frisked her with his gaze, catching sight of a trim ankle and her hot-pink polished toes peeking from fur-tipped slippers. That landed him a kick in the groin, and he groaned, nearly doubling over.

She must've heard, but except for a subtle misstep, she continued to twirl to the rhythm, the feathers following her every move. A flick of her wrist at the right beat and the fan wavered, allowing him a glimpse of a shapely thigh.

Luring him in.

He edged forward, caught himself, and reclined, stretching his arms across the back of the sofa, seemingly unaffected. Propping one leg across his knee, he paced her with his eyes, her reflection rippling in the mirrors.

Her hair, a shimmer of gold, fell down her back. The white silk a whisper across her hips...a flash of erotic shadow beneath.

A battering ram smashed him in the center of his chest, but by the time he inflated his lungs, the fan swung. He shifted his sights. The tie criss-crossing her cleavage loosened and the silk sagged, revealing the swell of her breasts. A smoldering began inside him; he spanned his hands across the velvet, itching to fondle, eager to taste, tease, nibble, suckle...her.

Easy man. The show's just getting started.

The smoldering torched his passion.

An inferno of sensation.

His shirt stuck to his shoulder blades. He swiveled a finger around his collar. How many other men had seen her...been turned on by the rhythmic movements of her body draped in that sexy scrap of *niente*. That did not sit well with Cade. No way.

Before he could regroup, she bounced up to him, tapped his chin with the tip of the fan, then drew it down his chest to his belt buckle. A hot beat…and she spun around, the silk flared around her hips, leaving nothing to the imagination.

Veins in his neck thickened and his pulse raced like a locomotive about to derail. How wrong could a guy be about the woman he loved? His sex kitten was a vamp.

He was about ready to blow a fuse.

A crescendo of sound, and she closed the fan. Flinging it behind her, she took a pose—hands crossed on slightly bended knees, a sexy pout on her mouth. Her scent drifted to him, subtle… sensual…womanly. Her nipples puckered beneath the silk, her breath a whisper of sound.

Sweat broke out across his forehead, and he clamped his hands behind his neck, his biceps bulging. She'd filled his hands and his mouth so perfectly. Blood rushed to his brain, then shot down, fueling his solid strength.

Cade crunched nails between his teeth.

The tune changed tempo, and she flashed him a smile. Stretching her arms above her head, she bopped a step back, her bosom bouncing and her hair flowing.

He tightened his abs and tasted metal on his tongue.

A note fused with sensual assault filled the air, and she turned, tossing him a sultry look over her shoulder; her sales pitch a purr of sound. "This fur trimmed shimmer of silk" –a bat of an eyelash, an inviting tone— "fire and ice…every woman's dream." She twirled, the material a hush against her hips, the shadow between—a forbidden promise. "And every man's fantasy—"

"Nightmare." Cade erupted from the couch, startling her and surprising himself.

"What's the matter?" She reached out, and stroked his jaw with her fingertips. "Can't take the heat?"

A muscle bashed his temple. "This fantasy is over, sweetheart." An inferno stoked inside him, his pulse clubbing his ribs.

"You don't like it?" She trailed the furry hem down his forearm, her gaze a mystery.

Cade liked it just fine. Too much. He wanted to do the caveman thing, but he had too much riding on this to tempt fate again and have it backfire. His gut wrenched. This five foot two dynamo had him for breakfast, lunch and dinner a year ago. Then on their wedding night, she had disappeared without a trace, leaving him to rebuild brick by brick, heartbeat by— well, it was time he leveled the playing field.

His eyes shuttered, camouflaging the firestorm inside him, his voice a thread of sound. "Before how many men have you paraded that sexy little number?"

"I run a reputable business."

"Sure thing, babe." He hooked his thumb at the snap of his jeans, his words laced with sarcasm.

"Oh!" Her eyes glittered with fury, and she wrapped the silk closer about her body, but that only hiked the fabric further up her hip. "You have no idea—"

"I'm willing to learn, sweetheart." He leaned into her and grazed the curve of her cheek with his knuckles.

She knocked his hand away and stepped back, her breath whooshing from her mouth.

Two paces more brought him within an inch of her, and he grinned in big bad wolf mode. "Maybe we should pursue this… uh…fantasy, after all?"

A heart-stopping moment, and Nina glimpsed iron-like flecks in his eyes. She caught her lip between her teeth, thinking she may have gone too far in provoking him. "What do you mean?"

"What happens next, doll?"

"Well, I…uh…that depends on…" She flicked a strand of hair off her shoulder, and swallowed her nervousness. Could she carry out the ruse? And remain unscathed?

"Yes?" He lowered his head, his lips a feather breadth from hers, his breath a warm caress upon her cheek.

The melody tempted, and he pulled her into a waltz. The rough fabric of his shirt stimulated her breasts, his thighs flirted with hers and his arousal courted her. They circled once around the floor, and he stopped, sliding the silk straps off her shoulders. He dipped his head and licked the hollow of her collarbone.

A hum in her throat, and she tilted her head back, allowing him further access. His hands glided down her arms, thumbs caressing inner flesh until he caught her fingertips. He brought them to his lips, then placed them on his shoulders, and spanned her waist with his hands. A crescendo of sound, and he toured upward, untying the ribbon at the décolleté of her negligee until her breasts filled his palms.

She held her breath.

A rumble came from deep inside him.

She exhaled, arching into him, her hands sliding through his hair. He lowered his head, pulled a nipple into his mouth and sent a myriad of sensation throughout her body. Her moan of pleasure mingled with his groan of need, and she embarked on a quest of discovery across his body. While he nibbled upward, feasting on her every curve, every pulse point, her fingers stumbled onto his surging strength. He heaved in a gallon of air, his head buried in the crook of her neck, and exhaled a gale.

The clock in the shop chimed the sixth hour, seeming to echo a warning, and startled, she let him go. A tremor zinged through her.

"I can't do this, Ca-ade." She shook her head, sucked a mouthful of air, and let it fizz between her teeth. "I-I really can't do this."

"You seemed to be doing fine, a minute ago," he panted into her neck.

"Aren't you forgetting y-your special lady?"

"She knows all about it," he muttered, his words muffled by her hair.

"Wha-at?"

"She'll understand, Nina."

"No woman in her right mind would—"

He chuckled into her nape. "If she's your mo—"

She shoved him back, but he barely budged, only a couple of inches separating them. "You're wacko," she snapped, hiding her quivery fingers behind her back. "Working in the Italian sun must have blistered your brain."

A tense beat, then he tossed back his head and laughed.

"Get away from me." She hobbled backward, bumped into the sofa and groped behind her for the armrest to regain her balance. "I'm getting changed."

"I'll help you—"

She held up her hand.

"—with the zipper," he huffed the words out.

"No, thank you." With a toss of her head, she glided out, the silk swishing upward, giving him a glimpse of the gold thong decorating her derriere.

Cade muttered an expletive that would've made even his construction crew cringe. This was not going well. Every cell in his body was stimulated and his muscled length throbbed...for her. He seized his hardhat off the carpet and stomped after her, detouring to the counter.

"Okay then, finish the wrap job." He plunked the hat on the counter and drummed his fingers on it, ignoring the rumble in his chest. He'd like her wrapped in deep purple satin sheets, pulsing beneath him— "And wrap the red in a separate box."

Silence.

He rang the bell. "I've paid plenty for that scrap of nothing."

No response.

He kept his finger on the buzzer.

A gold slipper sailed over his head.

"I want—"

"Go to—" The second pump came flying, and he ducked in the nick of time. It crashed in the display window and knocked down a mannequin draped in a multitude of sensual delights.

She dashed out of the dressing room, wiggling into her dress which still rode high on her hips and skidded to a stop. "What have you done?"

"*Moi?*" Face all innocence.

She pulled the dress down her thighs, but the hem snagged on her bracelet. "O-o-oh!"

For a moment, he watched her wrestle with the material, then his gaze strayed to her most vulnerable places; curves he touched, tasted, hungered for—his chest grew tight, reflecting a lower part of his anatomy. He wanted her…more of her…all of her.

"May I?" he offered.

"No!" She yanked at the crepe cotton and when it tore away from the gold chain at her wrist, she hurried back, returning a second later with the negligee bunched in her hands. She stuffed it in the giftbox, slammed on the lid and marching fast-forward, shoved it at him. "I hope you'll be very happy."

"That was the idea." He scratched his head, and his lips twitched. "Especially since she's already married to m—"

"She's married?" Nina stuttered, her emotions fried. Oh gosh, she was going to die. Pass out right in front of him. And she mustn't. At least, not until after he left. She clutched the counter before her legs gave out and she slithered to the floor. "Have you no morals?"

"Apparently not in your opinion," he muttered, his words a splinter of sound, eyes glinting hard.

"*Arrivederci,*" she murmured, swallowing the quiver in her voice. "I'm done."

"I'm not." He swept up the gift box and stomped to the exit. "I'll pick up the red tomorrow."

"No!"

"Actually, yes," he bit out. "I'll come and claim what I paid for."

Blinking angry tears away, Nina spun around so fast she stubbed her toe on the leg of the glass-topped table in the corner. "Ow!" She dove to save the vase toppling onto the floor, missed, and knocked over the display rack. Sprawled flat on her face on the carpet with an array of sensual accessories—frilly bikinis, embroidered thongs, lacy garters, soaps, scents, lotions, creams, glosses, glitter, toys strewn about her, did nothing for her dignity.

"You all right?" Cade dumped the gift box on the settee by the exit and hurried to her.

"Go away." An embarrassed flush sheathed her body, her heart careening down a precipice, and her only reprieve, the ceiling fan sending a current of cool air her way.

"Nina?" Cade touched her shoulder, and when she didn't move, fear whipped through him. "Hey, are you okay?"

She went ballistic, swinging her arms and kicking her legs, silks and soaps flying every which way. "Go!"

"Hold on, now." He dodged her flailing hands and lifted her to her feet.

"O-o-o-h," she squealed, pushing him away. "What kind of man are you?"

That did it. He tightened his jaw. Exhausted after a grueling day at the site, he'd come to her, hoping that maybe...*a reality check, man.* She'd driven him from the heights to the depths and every level in between since he arrived. Enough. What kind of man was he?!

"This kind." He hauled her into his arms and kissed her with a fervor that left her breathless and, him panting for more.

When finally he broke the contact, they swallowed heaps of air, arms interlocked, eyes at a tug-of-war. That lasted for a nanosecond, and then he plundered her mouth, his tongue mating in a frenzy with hers, swirling, licking, tasting...peppermint candy.

A rasp of sound deep in his throat. He curved his hand on her nape, his fingers caressing her skin, his mouth sliding across her cheek, a hush of a breath in her ear, his teeth tugging at her earlobe; and then he kissed his way to her chin, down her neck, his tongue flicking the pulse point at the base of her throat.

"Cade?"

"Shh," he murmured, working his way back to her mouth.

She locked her arms around his neck, fingers weaving a fevered tempo through his hair, her foot brushing his leg.

"Little darlin."

"Mmm, big guy."

He smiled against her lips and slipping the crepe fabric off her shoulders, exposed her breasts. A dip of his head, and he took a shadowed crown into his mouth, his tongue courting the nipple to erection. A guttural sound in his throat pulsed in sync with her purr of pleasure. In a fever, he unzipped his jeans and pushed her dress above her hips.

"Cade...."

"Shh, honey. Almost there."

He lifted his head and pillaged her mouth, his hand fondling her breast, his thumb grazing the nipple. Downward he traveled, across her abdomen, his hand bumping the trinket at her navel, then sliding lower, his fingers gliding over her moist core.

Bracing himself against the counter, he hoisted her up and anchored her against his hips. She locked her legs around him, and he plunged inside her, her warm folds enfolded him; he thrust into her again and again.

Sweet, sweet pleasure.

He caught her moan of desire in his mouth, his tongue creating a mating cadence of its own, and rode her deep and fast and high. Digging her hands into his shoulders, she cried his name, but his tongue swept it up. He held onto her on the climb, suspended for a moment, sweet little death...

She burst into multiple sensations, as he exploded.

Surfing the pulsing wave with her, he dropped his head onto the crook of her shoulder, humbled. "Dear God, Nina."

"Oh, Cade," she murmured, sliding her limbs down his length until her toes touched the carpet. Brushing moist curls off his brow, she slid her fingertip down his temple and across his cheek, the stubble rough beneath her touch; but she didn't care, moving to his mouth. She outlined his lips, and he nipped...she drew in a sharp breath, and he pulled her finger into his mouth, licking, stroking, suckling, making her gasp with delight.

He pressed his lips to her palm, cupped her buttocks, and pulled her smack against his hips. The impact knocked her off balance, and she tumbled with him onto the carpet behind the counter, her muffled giggle mingling with his muted chuckle.

Nina curled her toes into the carpet, and placed a kiss on his neck, tasting the salt of his sweat-damp skin. Her hands traveled down his body, unbuttoning and spreading his shirt open, her mouth following the hot trail of her fingers. She skimmed the fuzz on his chest with her lips, and his cologne—the hint of cool spice—rocked her heart off course. Her fingertips tormented one flat nipple, then her mouth settled over it, her tongue teasing it pebble-hard. A growl echoed in his throat, and she smiled, pleased.

Her hands toured down the stream of dark hair to his navel and beyond, until his prize filled her palms. She stroked, flirted, fondled. A breath, and her mouth traveled lower, wanting to love every inch of this man who was her destiny.

With a gut-wrenching groan, he squeezed her shoulders, putting a check to her desire. Her hand stilled. He lifted her face to his, gold flecks glittering in his brown gaze, reflecting the firestorm inside him. "There's no going back."

Her heart slammed against her ribs and an air pocket caught in her throat. "I-I know."

He surged in her hands and, blasted a breath that came out a heavy groan. "Who am I to you?"

She curved her lips in a timeless smile. "You are…"

He tightened his hands over her shoulders. "Say it."

"My husband."

He chucked her chin with his knuckles. "And don't you forget it."

Joy welled up inside her, then everything flashed through her mind, and she turned quiet, her elation dimming. A thousand questions bombarded her brain even in the heat of passion.

"What's wrong?"

"You were shopping for a bride…in my boutique."

"Sure was," he confessed, grinning. "The sexy one was for you, and the red for my mother…the other woman I love."

"Another con, Cade?" she murmured, but there was a lilt to her words.

"I had to do something drastic to get a reaction from you."

She smiled. Somehow she'd known, but had resisted against it. But no more.

"I had to know, to confirm what I've believed." He cupped her cheek, his thumb stroking the corner of her mouth.

"And what did you believe?" She splayed her hand across his chest, his heart pounding beneath her palm, her fingers flirting with the sprinkle of hair on his chest, his nipple.

A torrent of air rushed from his lungs, a tense beat and, "You… uh…feel me deeply."

"Sure?"

"Yeah." He laughed. "Yeah." He bent his head, his mouth a hair-breadth from her own. "Say it, wife."

She kept her counsel, her hand rerouting down his torso… his muscles flexed…a tickle at his navel, and she inched lower, spiking his desire.

"Nina, admit it," he demanded, his words a low rumble.

"Let's see…"

And so, Cade had no choice but to go on the offensive. His fingers feathered her inner thigh, and his mouth settled over her breast, his tongue coaxing the nipple to a hard nub. She sucked in a mouthful of oxygen, exhaled a blissful sound, and held his head to the spot. His hand dallied at her bosom, then strayed to her midriff, sensitizing nerve endings and toured her belly button on approach to a lower landing.

She shut her eyes. "Mmm, good."

"You have something to confess?"

"I do." She peeked at him from beneath her lashes, a pixie smile on her mouth. "I'm craving a tall mocha frap."

"You're what?" Astounded, Cade spanned his hand across her abdomen and heard her indrawn breath. Okay, she must be feeling him with that reaction…good, he was still in control.

"You can have one too."

"Gee, thanks." He chuckled. "But I'll trump your offer, lil' darlin'."

"I don't see how."

"A Broadway show after—"

"The Lion King?" she was quick to insert.

"Sure, why not?" He brushed her bottom lip with his thumb and tenderness nicked his heart. He wanted to give her the world but only if he came with it.

"Oh, Cade," she sighed. "You are the love of my life."

"Bout time," he grumbled and smiling against her mouth, closed the sweetheart of a deal.